THE PRIESTESS

AND THE

RAVENKNIGHT

"How long have you been doing this, High Priestess?" I asked, feeling more relaxed now that we were alone.

"Quite a long time," she answered calmly. "My thanks for allowing me to finish my task with the wood elf. I did wonder how long you would stand there and watch." The high priestess turned and gazed up at me with her dark azure eyes. She looked so proud and fearless, but mayhap, also, a bit unsure about what to do next.

I know I was. Her beauty rendered me speechless until I realized she was frowning. Afore I could utter a reply, she stood up in haste, and stepped away from the fiery pit, her eyes never leaving mine. I stepped back when I saw her extend her right hand, which held her sceptre, turning the ornate rod into a full-length staff that glimmered in the firelight. She whispered a quick incantation that made her entire body shimmer. Poised to attack, she lifted up her staff, aiming its sharp point at my chest.

Sir Krymson's Prayer

Where can you be? Where are you now? Do you not hear us scream?
Will you not hither come this day to end his wicked scheme?
'Tis wrong, so wrong and must be stopped, but I am only one.
My duty forces me to kill and challenge everyone.
Must I forsake my knightly vows to never harm or steal?
Should I arrest those wretched souls regardless how I feel?
My city, once a radiant jewel beside the Rhinestone Pier
Is lost to a new god so cruel that reigns now without fear.
Have you not seen his thirst for blood and deadly daimonae?
The prison's full of innocents that could not get away.
What must I do to help the weak that hide both day and night
When orders bid me to arrest thy followers on sight?
What can I do for Espion, so it is like afore?
Should I betray, serve you alone, a ravenknight no more?
Alas, dear goddess, are you there? I beg you on my knees.
Come free us with thy mighty power. Help us, if you please.

Thy servant now and always, Krymson

The Priestess and the Ravenknight

Written & Illustrated
by E.V. Medina

Book I of the World of Tiaera Trilogy

Never lose hope in Love.

E. V. Medina
Oct 2021

Dragonling Treasures

Lake Havasu City, AZ

www.Dragonling.com

Book design & illustrations by E. V. Medina

Copyright © 2015 by E. V. Medina - All rights reserved

4th Edition

ISBN-13: 978-1492219682

ISBN-10: 1492219681

Author's Note: Some of the words, spellings and capitalizations used throughout this book are intentionally not consistent with modern English usage in order to reflect the characters' dialects and accents. I have also used a UK dictionary for character dialogs. The characters and events portrayed in this book are fictitious. Any similarity to real persons, living or dead, is coincidental and not intended by the author.

Printed in the USA

Dedication

To the gallant men,
Matt McQuinn, Jon Blunk and Alex Teves,
who sacrificed their lives to protect the women
they loved at an Aurora Movie Theatre
in Colorado on July 20, 2012. I dedicate this tale
to honor their memory and to thank them for
affirming that courage and chivalry still
exist in this modern age.

Acknowledgments

Thanks to my friends Vince, Kelley and Amanda who
helped me with editing and proofreading this story. A
big thanks to my parents and husband for their patience
and encouragement to keep writing.

The Cathedral of Espion

Chapter 1

It all began when my captain felt 'twould be wise to have a number of foot soldiers and several ravenknights at the great Cathedral of Espion in case of any trouble by disguised loyalists of Goddess Astria. The Mother Goddess, as she was also known, was once the city's beloved deity and not everyone was prepared to give up their faith despite facing arrests and inquisitions which often condemned those unfortunate souls to Eternal Death.

The thought of such a fate disturbed me greatly for I had tasted the void of darkness I have come to know as *death* afore being summoned back to life by a druid's resurrection ritual and the goddess' blessing. To die with no hope of resurrection must be unbearable, especially for young dark elves like me. I had many decades of life to live, not to mention dreams to fulfil.

To avoid such an execution, many of the local druids and citizens fled the country as soon as they learned of the official dispossession of the goddess and the defilement of her cathedral. Many locked up their shops packed their belongings in order to board ships for Athrylle afore they were arrested. Others rebelled as much as they dared till they were forced to hide.

I witnessed it all and even did my duty as commanded despite the inner turmoil of my conscience. As a ravenknight, my duty was to assist the city militia to control unruly crowds and arrest rioters in the streets to keep order.

Though I was not accustomed to going to services or even praying, I grew up believing in the Mother Goddess, silent and unseen as she was, as the creator of Tiaera and the guardian of us all. But life had changed and Espion would, henceforth, belong to a new deity known as Ludovique Firebrand, the Disciple of Wrath.

As I stood inside the great cathedral, I looked up at the grey stone walls, rib-vaulted ceilings and smooth pillars and silently wished the ceremony would end. The smell of incense and the chanting of the congregation completed the uneasy experience as I caught sight of the huge candle-lit statue of Ludovique at the main altar. 'Twas very tall and hideous and it had enormous bat wings. There were spikes all over it and horns on his head. Part creature and part human, 'twas an unnatural abomination, the like I had never seen afore. No one knows whence he came or how, but one look at him and the bat-like creatures that acted as his henchmen forewarned that darker days were yet to come.

Did I volunteer to stand guard at the worship services out of guilt or curiosity? Well, 'twas a little of both. I had heard the enormous statue of the goddess was gone as well as paintings and flowers that the druids and followers brought to decorate the sanctuary. 'Twas true, all true and to my surprise, disheartening. I had no right to feel anything, but I did. And the guilt over my involvement as a ravenknight burned my soul. The threat of facing Eternal Death, if I did not follow orders, was that strong. I suppose I could have fled the city like the others, but I was not ready to abandon everything. Being a dark elf and a ravenknight gave me some time to plan for a new life outside Sangrey aforehand, in case it became too dangerous even for me.

So this was what we had come to? Oh, Goddess Astria, where were you? Had you forsaken us without a fight? Why did you not come and vanquish this scoundrel? Oust him and those demons he calls the Host of Wrath, those *daimonae* that feed on our flesh if we fail to obey.

I suddenly realized I was not just thinking, but mayhap even praying! A sudden pain filled my heart as the words of my prayer flooded my mind. Could Ludovique hear my thoughts and prayers? I swallowed hard and gripped the hilt of my sword, ready to jump if attacked. This was considered blasphemy and subject to arrest or worse. I looked everywhere around the sanctuary for any sign or appearance of the god or his black, nightmarish daimonae.

But nothing happened.

The congregation waved their hands in worship, their voices calling out to Ludovique the way they used to for the goddess. The air inside was thick with the odours of unwashed bodies, candle wax and most of all, fear. I could see it in their faces even as they prayed for the new god's blessings.

My heart slowed and the grip on my sword relaxed. I surmised he could *not* hear my thoughts and prayers, or mayhap he was busy elsewhere and luck was with me. But alas, I heard naught from the goddess as well. I cursed under my breath feeling abandoned and forlorn even though I was never a faithful worshiper. But I knew I would do far less for Ludovique.

Resigned to my fate under the new god, I patiently waited for the service to continue as planned. I rubbed my eyes and tried to concentrate once more on the task at hand. Our orders were to stand guard and arrest anyone interfering with the ceremony conducted by High Priestess Azurene V'Nae. Having heard of her beauty from some of my brethren, I chose to stand in the side aisle by one of the pillars near the chancel.

'Twas thither I first beheld her as she entered, followed by several other members of the clergy, and took her place at the altar. Anger swept over me as I thought about the way she had turned her back on the goddess to save herself from persecution and retain her position as a high priestess. I knew very little about her. Rumours reached me about her lust for blood, and yet she was a personage of high regard to the citizens of Espion. Or was this regard based on fear of persecution? In reality, as Ludovique's high priestess, she was naught but a beautiful coward and heretic, as far as I was concerned. Then I realized I was not much different from her. Was I not doing the same to avoid persecution? How could I condemn her without knowing all the facts? My disdain waned as I thought about this. Hence, I listened as she began her sermon and after a time, found myself watching her more than I should have.

She was quite lovely indeed, dressed in a priestly robe that hid her feminine charms, too well. Her face looked youthful and ageless as is typical of our race. But I had to remember she was the new High Priestess of Wrath. I wondered what the high priestess' part in all this was. That matter truly vexed me.

How could someone so beautiful be so evil? Does she not know what this god had wrought? Could she not see the misery and sorrow of our people? Cursed witch! I continued to scorn her. I wanted to loathe her with all my heart and I tried, truly tried to do so.

Dark elves are good at summoning the hatred and fury needed to survive. We are not so bad at holding grudges too. 'Tis in our nature and I am no exception. Once an enemy, always an enemy and it takes much to change that. But alas, I was commanded to protect her; not vanquish her. But I wanted her to cease beguiling me with her beauty. And 'twas all I could do to remember where I was, standing like some imbecile, feeling stiff in my ravenknight armour.

The gold and silver symbols of her robe reflected the light of the candelabras as she moved with grace. Priestess Azurene's voice was clear and somewhat melodious to my ears. In silence I sought to distract myself of her influence by turning my head to look upon all the dark elves seated in the pews. I beheld mothers holding their babes and young children standing at their feet. No humans. No gnomes or halflings. All were dark elves like me.

'Twas so hard to believe she worshipped the monstrous idol close by. I pondered the notion of confronting her after the ceremony. Was it wise? Was she beguiling the other ravenknights in like manner? So many questions needed to be answered.

Her arms rose upward like that of a dancer whilst she prayed aloud. I sought to get a good look at her face, but her silk hood made that difficult. She seemed to hear my thoughts and turned her face in my direction. To my dismay, her dark eyes looked right at me with such sorrow, I blinked in disbelief. Something was amiss, but what? I gripped the hilt of my sword and looked at every pew in the sanctuary.

Could she be worrying about an assassin or a traitor hiding in the crowd? No one entered armed. The ravenknights made sure of that. Everyone was carefully checked for magic items and weapons. Every door had at least one ravenknight whilst others patrolled outside in case they were needed. Alas, what was it? Was it the presence of me and my men inside the sanctuary? If this is so, 'twill be hard to find a way to meet her in private, let alone convince her to return to the goddess.

Besides, who am I to even try to meet with her and talk about the goddess when my own faith is weak? If 'twere not, I would defy the new god and suffer Eternal Death with the same courage and devotion of the martyrs. Whilst I continued to ponder about this, the high priestess turned away to face the congregation and raise her hands.

"And now, all arise for The Offering," she said in a voice that sounded strange. She stepped to one side of the altar and bowed to the statue of

Ludovique. The other priests stepped forward as if to attend her in this ritual.

The congregation stood, eyes down and hands clasped in solemn reverence. Some were peasants whilst others were well-known merchants and scholars, but they all seemed resigned to this life we have to live under the new god.

"May this life please you enough to grant us thy favour and continued blessings. We trust in you, Dark Father and do this in thy name. Praise be, Ludovique Firebrand, Lord of Sangrey and one day... all of Tiaera!" The high priestess cried out at the unseen god then slowly removed a colourful shroud to reveal a young wood elf female, lying in some kind of trance upon the elaborate altar close by. After carefully folding the shroud, the high priestess handed it to one of the priests.

Nay! This could not be! I almost cried out, but managed to say naught, remembering why I came hither in the first place. My body tensed as I resisted stepping away from my station. Taking a deep breath, my eyes focused on the lovely pale female that did not move at all.

Everyone then watched as the priestess revealed a bejewelled dagger she was holding. Its steel blade reflected the candlelight, giving it an almost mystical aura. Her lips moved prayerfully just afore she suddenly drove the blade into the heart of a young wood elf.

Some of the faint-hearted in the congregation gasped, but that was to be expected. A child cried somewhere in the crowded sanctuary. Others simply looked away. Many still cringed over the need for sacrifice to Ludovique. It took all my discipline to stay at my station, silent and unmoved by the spectacle that had taken place.

The rumours were true! Murderous blasphemer! This was wrong, so wrong, and dare I say it, an act of sheer wickedness. The Mother Goddess *never* demanded sacrifices and yet this new god did. And as an Espion ravenknight, I was honour-bound to follow orders and watch an innocent die at the hands of my people. All I could do was close my eyes, but for a moment, and keep silent.

"Praise to you, Dark Father, Ludovique Firebrand! Champion of our race, lift us up as the elite nation we are meant to be. Accept our offering of blood and bone this night," cried the high priestess, turning her face upwards. Her eyes were brimmed with tears of lustful passion. No one could mistake that look.

"Praise our god and saviour!" answered the congregation. "Praise the mighty Ludovique!"

"Praise him indeed! Now go in peace and may the Dark Father bless you all until we meet again." The high priestess raised her bloodied hands with her palms outward in a gesture of blessing. People rose from their seats and headed for the front entrance of the cathedral. Now that the ceremonial sacrifice was over, human slaves appeared from behind the altar to carry the wood elf's body downstairs.

High Priestess Azurene looked pale and her eyes glistened in the candlelight. Would that I could comfort her in my arms at that very moment, but how? How could I comfort an *executioner* dressed as a holy lady of divine power? She was just like this cathedral: faultless on the outside, but evil on the inside. She was Ludovique's servant just as I was, but I was forced into his service and I would never worship him like she does. It was all too clear how she delighted in the murder of that helpless wood elf. She was evil! And that was the difference betwixt us.

I did vow one day I would escape from Espion and the dominion of this ... demon god and his vile servants. But an escape from the city required an abundance of coin and preparations. Whilst I prepare and save, there must be some way I can help such innocents like that wood elf. This is not the first sacrifice and it shan't be the last.

But alas, who is going to trust a ravenknight?

There must be a way to help! 'Till then, I needed to learn more about the high priestess. She had beguiled me beyond reason. 'Twas most important that my feelings for her were resolved afore leaving Espion and this would doubtless require a confrontation. Therefore, I lingered and watched her leave with the other clergy members whilst the acolytes in the sanctuary proceeded to put out the candelabras.

Timing was crucial so I hurried and ordered one of the other ravenknights to secure the front door once everyone had left, then I rushed back down the side aisle of the sanctuary to the south transept entrance. I waited to make sure everyone from the congregation left then closed and locked that door. The sanctuary was now empty.

Time to make my move if I was going to do this at all.

Chapter 2

Once everyone had departed, I sought to find the door where the clergy and slaves had taken the body. Upon finding the hidden door behind a tapestry, I opened it and went down the stairs. The wall sconces did a poor job of illuminating the passageway, but this enabled me to use the shadows to follow discreetly. Lurking in plate armour was almost impossible so I kept my distance and froze when needed to keep from being heard. I paused when I came upon a heavy wooden door. Peering carefully through a tiny opening, I beheld a torch-lit chamber that was round and empty of furnishings.

The priests chanted and prayed while the high priestess cast a fireball big enough to start a blaze inside a large pit in the floor at the centre of the chamber. The slaves laid the body down next to it. It appeared as if she was going to push the corpse into the fire.

So this was the way they committed their sacrifices to Eternal Death! Merciful goddess Astria! Why do you not stop this? If you shan't, then I shall, or perish trying. I pondered what I would do afore bursting in. There were six priests and four slaves. I doubted the slaves would fight at all, but the priests and the high priestess had powerful spells and weapons.

'Twas then, I beheld the lady wipe her hands and dismiss everyone from the chamber. I could imagine that the stench of burning flesh was enough to send anyone out without question. Their abeyance clearly showed their trust in her. I quickly hid in the shadows once again until the priests and slaves went up the stairs. I stepped back to the opened door quietly, prepared to end this heinous ritual.

The priestess must have done this so many times she was getting careless, for I managed to enter unnoticed whilst her attention was on the dead wood elf. Kneeling by the young female's corpse, the priestess gently lifted up her head and shoulders then began waving her free hand slowly over the chest area where the dagger's blade had penetrated. Azurene appeared concerned, frowning even as she closed her eyes to concentrate. Her deep red lips moved in silent prayer or incantation. I know not which for certain.

My mind reeled with so much wonder and curiosity methinks I stopped breathing for a minute lest she realize she was not alone. I beheld neither blood nor any movement from the wood elf until the priestess finished her murmurings and opened her eyes. She beheld the wound once again and seemed pleased. I lowered my sword when after a minute or so, the wood elf opened her eyes.

"Forgive me. It had to be done," Azurene said with such a sincere tone in her voice. She helped the girl get to her feet. "How do you feel?"

"I live? But why, priestess? Was it not you who took my life?" The wood elf looked down and beheld the blood-stained tunic she wore with the hole where the dagger had cut through. Puzzled, the girl gazed up at the priestess for an answer. I believe she knew what had happened to her, but not why.

A Resurrection spell! I almost acted at that very moment, but resisted the urge, preferring to wait just a bit longer. Never was I so glad to be mistaken in my life. I wanted to shake my gauntlet fists and cheer, but I kept still so I could learn more about what was happening.

Indeed, I was wrong and truly glad of it. My spirit soared like a falcon in the sky over what I had witnessed. I smiled and silently thanked the goddess. I know not if this encounter was part of her plan, but I would like to think so. The Mother Goddess is ever mysterious as she is benevolent.

Moments later, Azurene pulled back her hood, revealing her long white hair that hung in waves from a tied ribbon. The tips of her pointed ears peeked through the loose tendrils that framed her soft blue complexion. For a dark elf, she was rather pale, suggesting there might be some human or high elf blood in her. It mattered not to me for her large eyes and burgundy lips aroused me once again. She had this effect on me above during the service and I felt it here again. I wanted her! I longed to run my fingers through her hair and touch her velvet-soft cheek, but timing was everything. I needed to wait just a few minutes more and then I had to be very careful. This gesture of mercy toward the wood elf could have been a trick. Alas, I reminded myself she was the High Priestess of Ludovique.

'Twas as if to ease my concern, I beheld Azurene embrace the wood elf and praise aloud the goddess Astria. Then the priestess pulled herself back to look into the wood elf's eyes, "I am sending you to Kyngeston City. Take this. Know you how to read?"

The wood elf looked down at the small note the priestess handed her. She frowned and said, "Nay, High Priestess. Kyngeston? But why? How?"

"Tarry not within the city, but seek out one of the Royal Mystics. Make haste to their guild hall and give them this message. Tell no one else about me! Understand?"

I understood completely. She was helping the young wood elf escape Espion. I had heard about the Royal Mystics of Kyngeston and was therefore intrigued. This was truly amazing. Such courage!

The wood elf's eyes filled with tears. 'Twas clear to see she was moved by the kindness of the dark elf priestess. The one that killed her, had brought her back to life and was now helping her to escape.

"Oh, thank you! Gramercy, High Priestess! May the Mother Goddess bless you and thy family for this kindness. I shall never forget you, milady," she cried. Tenderly, she embraced her heroine.

The scene afore me was quite moving, even for a hardened ravenknight like myself. I was truly glad I did this and I can imagine how my life would have turned out had I not done this.

The high priestess touched her own lips with an index finger and said, "I beseech you, say naught about me and what I just did to anyone. If I am found out, 'twill jeopardize the lives of other prisoners I can help in the future, not to mention what would befall me."

"I shan't say a word. I do vow never to fail you. May the Mother Goddess grant you the ability to save more lives and to give you whatever help you may need. Gramercy, milady."

"My thanks and farewell." Azurene smiled and stood up, helping the wood elf to her feet as she did. The priestess began her next incantation and pointed with her sceptre, creating a portal of tiny sparkling lights that formed a large circle in mid-air. The wood elf entered and disappeared, sending her out of the chamber. Where she went, I knew not, but that was of no importance. I waited afore doing anything until the mystical portal disappeared as well.

At last, with the wood elf now gone, I could keep silent no more. I took several steps towards her so she could see me better by the light of the torches. I did not draw my sword as I did not want to alarm her in any way.

"How long have you been doing this, High Priestess?" I asked, feeling more relaxed now that we were alone.

"Quite a long time," she answered calmly. "My thanks for allowing me to finish my task with the wood elf. I did wonder how long you would stand there and watch." The high priestess turned and gazed up at me with her dark azure eyes. She looked so proud and fearless, but mayhap, also, a bit unsure about what to do next. I know I was.

Her beauty rendered me momentarily speechless until I realized she was frowning. Afore I could utter a reply, she stood up in haste, and stepped away from the fiery pit, her eyes never leaving mine. I stepped back when I beheld her extend her right hand, which held a sceptre, turning the ornate rod into a full-length staff that glimmered in the firelight. She whispered a quick incantation that made her entire body shimmer.

Poised to attack, she lifted up her staff, aiming its sharp point at my chest.

This was not at all what I expected.

Chapter 3

Did I have a fight on my hands? How could this be so? The only thing I wanted to do right then was to talk to her. We were alone at last and to my delight, I had discovered we had more in common than I ever realized. I could not resist a smile whilst I raised my hand, palm out.

"A moment, if you please." I quickly checked the door to make sure no one else was about. I even used my helm's enchanted visor to look for anyone using a spell or talisman to make themselves invisible. Once I was sure we were quite alone, I closed the door and tried to smile. "Priestess, fear not. I came hither not to fight nor even arrest you. Quite the contrary, I would know more about you. Why did you save the female? Does Ludovique wish you to revive whomever you sacrifice? If so, 'tis a strange ritual indeed!"

"Nay! I did my part to satisfy Ludovique by taking her life in public, but I still have the power to revive her, and others like her, down here where I am usually alone. She deserves to live, sir."

I could see she was not at all pleased by my presence. I ignored her glare and tried some flattery. "I am most impressed that such a genteel female like thyself would have the courage to defy a god like Ludovique, even in secret."

The priestess lowered her staff and relaxed, although she kept her distance. "I only do whatever I must to help our people, Sir ...?"

"Krymson Larolin, milady. And you are High Priestess Azurene V'Nae; the one I just witnessed sacrificing a female wood elf and praying to a god that looks like death itself. Are you not afraid he will find out what you are doing here after the service? Are you certain he is not watching us at this moment?"

"Methinks he cannot or cares not. As I said afore, I have done this for some time. I can no longer continue to see innocents of any race be treated like animals. We call ourselves civilized and superior," she added, "then tell me why we murder for a god who has our people in his grip so tightly we are even killing our own just to please him?"

I did not answer right away, but looked down at the pit with its flames illuminating her in golden flickering light. She was right. I had recently come to that same conclusion. A part of me wanted to rejoice over the knowledge that she was not a willing priestess of the dark lord. But another part was suddenly concerned that she was risking her own life to live in Espion by posing as a devout priestess, doing as Ludovique commands. My heart swelled with admiration for her and her courage.

I should not have been so surprised that she was doing this. We dark elves are intelligent, educated and respected, mayhap even admired by the other races of Tiaera. That being said, there were some of us who felt slighted by the Mother Goddess, who seemed to favour the light-skinned beings of our world. On the rare occasions she ever appeared, she was tall and fair-skinned like the high elves.

Then Ludovique Firebrand came to our capital and convinced our city leaders he was a god like Astria. My commanding officers informed us that he could empower us to be the greatest army in all of Tiaera. He would show us how to be free of Astria's yoke so that we could fulfil our true destiny as befitting our noble race.

Laws were passed and those who did not accept the new god of Sangrey were expeditiously terminated. *Murdered* was more like it. Alas, 'twas all true for I had to do some of the killing myself. Down came the images and statues of Goddess Astria and orders were given to all ravenknights to ensure all but dark elves left the country or be put to Eternal Death.

Fear and death took over the city as my fellow ravenknights and I searched each household. Whole families were destroyed if they did not leave the country, abandoning their livelihood and homes. Mothers pleaded for the lives of their children if they were discovered and arrested. The rich tried to bribe us for safe passage. The poor could not afford the passage by ship or enarch, so they fled into the countryside, outside the safety of the city walls.

During one of my searches, I found a whole family of gnomes hidden in a dirt cellar beneath a large workbench. The fear in their eyes when they beheld me, filled me with shame. The parents grasped their little ones tightly. They were hardworking citizens who only wanted to live and prosper like anyone else. I gestured to keep silent and they nodded. I left them thither unharmed and unwilling to arrest them.

No hero am I. The goddess expected no less of me. 'Twas hard to trust anyone, but I had to try to help somehow. And I was not alone. 'Twas encouraging to hear that other dark elves helped fugitives escape by ship, enarch or magic portals. Friends and neighbours rallied to hide and protect each other in and out of Espion.

But then there were times where I had to prove I was loyal to my commanders and the new god. I tortured and killed in the name of Ludovique. My victims wailed and screamed as my men and I carried out their executions. No male, female or child was granted mercy. 'Twas was not long thereafter the killing made it hard to even sleep.

I drank at the local taverns until I could not bear it any longer. Taverns and ale houses were good places to hear about the goings-on of the city. There was talk that some conjurers, who supported the new god, were creating creatures never seen afore in Tiaera. They used the dark arts to distort the Ritual of Resurrection into creating beings who were undead, a term I had never heard afore. As 'twas explained to me, such magic did not require the goddess' blessing as the dead were not, in truth, living and normal again. Indeed, they moved and threatened anyone with sickness similar to that of the plague.

I had to do something within my means and no longer rely on the goddess to help us. Until I could find who these conjurers were or destroy their means to practice their dark magic, I had to find a way to save more lives. At night, disguised as a rogue, I did smuggle several humans and gnomes to stowaway on ships or ride by horseback for a chance to live. 'Twas not because I cared for the humans or the other races that came hither to Espion, but to kill them just because this new power said so? What about the elderly? And of the children? And what did sacrificing do for this god and our people?

At last, I answered the priestess. "I have been asking the same thing myself. In truth, I cannot arrest you for what you have just done, but this is no place to talk further. If we value our lives, we should go to some place safe where we can talk more about what has come to pass. You have to trust in me, milady. I would not have thy blood on my hands now when I... "

Azurene looked a bit surprised. "What? Speak! Be this some kind of trickery, sir? I shan't go with you anywhere this night or any other. I know naught about you and cannot risk you turning me in to the sheriff or thy commanding officers. I am a high priestess and as I can heal and revive, I can destroy. Alas, 'tis a pity we met this way for now that you know my secret, one of us must *die*."

"Wait! Nay!" I demanded. But no sooner did she speak, she made her attack. The priestess moved towards me with both hands on her staff as she pointed the end with the small cloud-filled sphere at me. It began to turn quickly and change colours. My normal reflexes are almost supernatural, but not when I am wearing my plate armour. When she shot a fireball from her staff, I moved as fast as I could. The fireball was no bigger than an apple, but its force sent me flying backwards, so that I smashed through the wooden door and landed on my backside against the hallway wall. I did open my eyes, stunned, but still alive because my armour was as enchanted as my weapons. No ravenknight would ever be caught on duty without such protection. There are far too many magic users in Espion and the rest of the world, for that matter.

My temper rose as I got to my feet, still teetering slightly. Though the fireball did not wound me, I did have trouble breathing from the blow. "Were you anyone else, milady,..." I murmured, fighting the urge to draw forth my sword. I had been a ravenknight for decades then and I had never raised my sword to a priest afore. And at that moment, more so than ever, was not the time to start.

Looking back up at her I thought I noted a hint of regret in her eyes, but I was once again mistaken. Alas, 'twas her fury that shined brightly in my direction. I was utterly lost as to how I should handle this situation. How could I make her understand that I was no threat afore 'twas too late and one or both of us ended up dead? At that moment I pictured her killing me and pushing my dead body into the fiery pit, out of reach from anyone who could bring me back to life. I had to do something whilst I still could!

"Priestess, prithee stop! On my word as a ravenknight, I shall neither fight nor harm you, not now, not ever, if possible." I raised my visor, hoping she could see I was earnest. The word of a ravenknight was highly regarded in Espion. 'Twas part of our code of chivalry that every ravenknight vowed to follow upon being bestowed their knighthood.

"As you will, ravenknight," she answered. "I truly regret it must end this way, but you must see that I have no choice. Too many lives are at stake over this encounter."

Afore I could utter another word, she came towards me and raised her staff again. I only had time to brace myself for the next blow. Instinctively, I closed my eyes and prepared for her onslaught.

Seconds later, when naught happened, I opened my eyes to see her shaking her staff with both hands. 'Twas not glowing anymore. The priestess looked puzzled and 'twas all I could do to keep from smiling. Stepping through the shattered doorway, I then paused several feet away from her, drawing my sword slowly.

"Fie upon it! Stand back, or I shall ..." She tossed aside her staff and waved her arms, reciting the words of a spell. Her bejewelled fingers all pointed towards me, but naught happened again. She was quite alarmed. Although her body still shimmered from the protective spell she thought she needed, it appeared she was powerless at that moment. I daresay, another lady might have swooned or had broken into tears at the time, but not Azurene. Her honour as a dark elf forbade it. Instead, she took a few steps back and drew her ceremonial dagger.

"Hand-to-hand combat? With me?! With naught but a dagger?!" I sighed heavily, removed my helm then laid it and my sword on the ground. "Enough! You have naught to fear from me, milady. I seek not thy wrath, but thy favour." I watched her turn the dagger to and fro as she did with the staff, but it behaved like any other normal dagger.

" 'Tis the Mother Goddess," she blurted, stunned by what just happened. She looked around the chamber anxiously. "Naught but the blessed Astria can remove my powers at will. It seems you, ravenknight, have *her favour*."

Her words stunned me and made me wonder. Could it be so? Does Astria favour me for some reason, after all I have done in the past? How can this be?

"Krymson, milady. And thank the goddess I do, though I know not why, as yet." I tried to smile, feeling strange and silly. "Prithee, I only wish to talk, but not here. Let us away anon."

"As you will, Krymson, but only because of what I have just been through." The priestess nodded, lowering her voice to a more genteel tone. And as if to confirm what she had said, we both beheld her staff on the ground suddenly glow with a flash of light. Upon seeing that, the priestess returned her dagger to the sheath that was hidden within the folds of her robe. "Merciful goddess, I do pray 'tis you."

Together, we went over to the staff and simultaneously bent down to pick it up. 'Twas at that moment our hands touched. I still wore my plate gauntlets, but it did not seem to matter, for when we touched I felt a strange yet wonderful sensation deep inside. 'Twas somewhat magical indeed, and I shall never forget it.

I let her take the staff, noting how small and delicate her hands were. She looked up at me and I had to wonder if she felt the same as I did. Afore I could ask, I noticed her eyes were no longer inflamed with alarm or filled with contempt. As close as we were, 'twas easy to see her look upon me with a faint blush on her cheeks and a rather shy and congenial smile.

"Milady, did you... " I started to ask when I realized we were no longer alone.

"My word! What has happened to this door?" A priest poked his head inside, assessing the damage afore turning his gaze towards us.

Chapter 4

We rose up and turned to face the priest. He appeared to be unarmed, but as I well know, looks can be most deceiving. My mind struggled to come up with a good explanation. I took a deep breath and gritted my teeth to keep from saying anything that could make matters worse. The priest turned his head to check the chamber once more, then lifted his robe slightly to step over the broken pieces of the door and enter.

He was dressed in a plain dark brown robe with a simple leather belt and boots. I could not make out what order he was from as he wore no brooch or medallion. Without his hood on, 'twas easy to see his dark greyish face, framed by his long, straight white hair that was tied back, much like mine. I looked over at the priestess who was also surprised until she seemed to recognize him, then she relaxed again and even smiled.

"There was a slight *misunderstanding*, Brother Tomiss," she explained. "I fear 'twas I who caused the damage. This ravenknight witnessed what I did, and I felt compelled to silence him forever. Allow me to introduce to you Ravenknight Krymson Larolin. I have been *compelled* to do him no harm by the goddess herself. It seems he can be trusted with what he has learned, for now. Is that not so?" The priestess looked up at me asking the question as if 'twere a challenge. It became evident that Brother Tomiss was an ally, so I relaxed and spoke freely.

"With my life, I do vow I shan't fail you and, henceforth, endeavour to assist you in thy work," I answered calmly, but with much conviction.

Brother Tomiss smiled, "I am honoured to meet you, Sir Larolin, but let us away anon. We know not who else remains in the cathedral this night."

"Indeed, I could not agree with you more, Brother Tomiss. But what about the damage to the door? Someone is bound to make inquiries," I replied, frowning at the priests.

"Then I shall explain that you came to this chamber unannounced and I was afraid you came hither to stop me from carrying out my duty as High Priestess. As we all know, you have no reason to be down here in the first place, and yet you are." Smiling, Azurene looked down at her glowing staff and with a slight twist of her wrist, it returned to the short sceptre it once was.

"Sister, allow me to contact the craftsmen about the door on the morrow." Brother Tomiss' eyes were bright from the firelight as he gestured towards the door. "And be at ease. If asked, I shall explain as you said. If I were alone down here and an armed ravenknight surprised me, I might have done the same. We druids cannot be too careful."

Then the priestess squinted as if to accuse me with her next question. "Which brings me to ask, why came you hither?"

I quickly explained my orders to them both, keeping brief and to the point. They seemed satisfied, but concerned as to how this was going to affect future ceremonies.

"We shall have to be ever vigilant. And what has become of the wood elf?" Brother Tomiss asked with a worried look.

"Gone," the priestess answered ominously.

"Splendid. And so should we, my friends. Let us tarry no longer." Brother Tomiss closed his eyes for a moment; a look of relief spread over his dark face. Gesturing to the doorway, he led us out of the chamber.

I did wonder how long this had been going on and who else knew about what really took place here. And what of Ludovique? If he is a god, would he not have witnessed what was happening to his sacrificial victims by now and therefore put a stop to it? Why has he not acted? Could it be he is not a real god? And if he is not, then what is he?

As I followed the druids out into the hallway and up the stairs, a strong desire to stay with Azurene a bit longer compelled me to ask, "High Priestess, if you please, allow me to escort you to thy abode. I have many questions about, well, about the new faith and Ludovique."

The priestess thought for a moment afore answering. "In view of what has happened, I do feel we have more to discuss. But I warn you, if thy intentions are not honourable, you shall see more of what my powers can do, and *no one* shall spare you then. Do we understand each other?"

"Aye, priestess, understood," I answered, unable to hide my grin. "On my word as a ravenknight, I shall do naught but talk and act as is fitting and proper."

She seemed pleased with my reply so we continued up to the main floor of the cathedral. I noticed everyone, including the ravenknights that had come with me earlier, were gone and indoors for the night. 'Twas quiet and the moonlight shone through the tall stained-glass windows as we walked the length of the sanctuary. The cloudy orb on the priestess' staff lit the path we walked until we got outside.

Not wishing to attract attention to ourselves, we continued our walk by the light of the moon. The road was littered and muddy as the three of us silently made our way towards our destination. I followed the two hooded druids, allowing them to walk ahead of me where I could watch them both. I did want to know more about her and I am certain she had more questions to ask of me. If we could come to some accord, mayhap we could build on this to benefit all those left here in Espion, committed to saving our people. I wanted to find out more about her faith and why she risked everything for a silent rarely-seen deity like Astria. And I would find a way to protect her from my superiors and any others who would do her harm.

Clouds began to fill the night sky, threatening rain. We heard the rumbling sounds of distant thunder, so we walked faster. 'Twas late and aside from a few revellers, who had been drinking, we met only the occasional sentry patrolling the streets. As I continued watching the hooded druids ahead of me, I began to wonder if this was a trap. 'Twas possible despite what had happened back at the cathedral. Anything is possible when it comes to druids and their magic.

I did not speak and thus hinder us from reaching our destination as quickly as possible. Instead, I turned my thoughts back to the goddess and glanced up at the sky, still hoping she was out there somewhere. I still could not believe she had intervened back at the cathedral when Azurene and I fought. Why there and not at the ceremony? She could have saved the wood elf. Where had she been when she was truly needed? I took a deep breath and spoke with my heart. I am but one dark elf, a knight, and a murderer. Why do I still live? Was it because you need me to help the high priestess and Brother Tomiss? Is Azurene thy true servant? Mother Goddess, if you still exist and can hear me, know I shall serve you still. Was it because you need me to help the high priestess and Brother Tomiss? Is Azurene thy true servant?

Mother Goddess, if you still exist and can hear me, know I shall serve you still.

As if he could read my thoughts, Brother Tomiss grinned and lowered his hood so we could see him better. "Good friends, the hour is late and so I shall depart anon. I would speak with you as soon as possible, sister, and fret not about the door. I shall see to it on the morrow."

"My thanks, gentle friend, and may the goddess keep you safe always," Azurene lowered her hood and embraced him is such a way that I felt a twinge of jealousy which I dismissed quickly.

When Tomiss turned and smiled at me, I did my best to look respectful and unaffected by the embrace. " 'Till then, be safe. Farewell, Sir Larolin. Mind thyself with the priestess. Were I not so confident in her powers I would stay. Until we meet again, bless you both and good-den."

I nodded. "You have naught to concern thyself. May our paths meet again, dark brother."

"Oh, I shan't and I am most certain one day they shall, Sir Larolin."

"So be it. I am at thy service and forswear never to reveal what I have learned this evening. Farewell, Brother Tomiss."

"I pray you shan't. Farewell."

The priestess embraced him once more; this time to whisper something to him that my keen ears could not understand. We watched him pull on his hood as drops of rain began to fall. He then stepped back a few paces and lifted up a blue crystal. In that moment, his illusion disappeared, showing us his true appearance: human.

I had orders to arrest anyone who was not a dark elf. And here I had thought him a good fellow until that moment! "Hold!" I commanded, drawing my sword, Runesaber. Tomiss stepped back and raised his hands.

"Krymson! Nay!" The priestess warned me, grabbing my elbow with both hands. "Smite him not! Stay thy hand!"

She was stronger than she looked as all dark elven females tend to be. I looked at her but for a moment, afore I turned back to the human, only to see him disappear into a wisp of tiny luminous stars that soared up into the cloudy sky till they were gone. That spell was familiar to me. Members of guilds use it, including myself. So I was certain he was safe somewhere, out of my reach.

"What folly is this? Know you not what kind of position you have put me in? You have deceived me. Why? Explain!" My words were laced with fury mixed with confusion as I turned to her.

The priestess did release my arm and stepped away from me. She pulled on her hood for the rain was falling harder. I did not do likewise, preferring to ignore the rain dripping down my face and helm with the hope 'twould help me control my anger. I stood frozen, watching her and trying to decide what to do. I so wanted to be with her and yet without trust, 'twas just too dangerous.

There was no one else about, but the two of us. And I was still pondering my next move when she suddenly pointed down the street and said, "He came to me at great risk when he thought I was in peril, Sir Larolin. I beseech you to calm thyself and follow. My abode is not afar. Let us go thither where we can get out of the rain and talk. On my word as Astria's priestess, I shall explain everything."

'Twas against my training and better judgment, but the look in her eyes, as she stood there in the rain, compelled me to follow. Was this part of the goddess' plan for me or part of my penance? Was she the answer to my prayers? I came to the conclusion that the only way I was going to find out what was in store for me was to risk everything I had to be with her this night. 'Twas not logic that drove me to this conclusion, but desire. I sorely wanted to be with her at all costs. Hence, I needed to either trust her and follow, or arrest her.

I could not arrest her.

Chapter 5

Though 'twas a rainy evening, I could see that the abode of Azurene V'Nae was attractive and well-kept, as would be expected of a high priestess. The two-story town house had a slate stone roof; the outer walls were white and framed with dark timber planks. Several expensive glass windows with wooden shutters adorned both the upstairs and downstairs, testifying to the wealth of their owner. As we approached the iron gate, I noticed a four-foot stone wall, sporadically covered with ivy and purple roses, that bordered her property and offered it relative privacy and protection without hindering the view of the charming town house from the street.

Anxious to get out of the rain, the priestess waved her hands and thus, unlocked the gate. We entered the front garden, stepping on a slate stone pathway. She waved her hands again as I heard the gate slam shut behind us, presumably locked once more. I made sure to remember this fact should I need to make a hasty retreat later. Fortunately, if all else fails and I need to make an escape, I have my guild's charm that will magically portal me from anywhere in Tiaera to the safety of my guild hall here in Espion.

"Stay behind me, Sir Larolin," she said, "at least until I have a chance to introduce you properly."

"Aye, milady." I nodded, expecting a nervous armed servant or mayhap a ferocious dog protecting his home. I was wrong on both accounts.

The priestess led me down the main pathway, lined by lit lamps to the front of the abode. Once there, she drew forth a intricate key and opened the door. Upon entering, I caught the fragrance of flowers nestled in a wooden basket by the door.

A metallic animated skeleton met us at the door. It stood almost six feet tall and its body gleamed from the candlelight. I daresay 'twould have looked attractive, were it not shaped like the skull and bones of a human. I had seen such afore when dealing with necromancers, but those were real skeletons of the dead. This one was a work of forged metal and magic. It even had the ability to speak.

"Good den, Humble. I have brought home a friend," Azurene said, turning to the skeletal servant. "His name is Ravenknight Krymson Larolin. Inform the others of him and bring us towels. He is not to be attacked or restrained unless I say otherwise."

"Good den, milady. Good den, sir," said the skeleton. "My name is Humble. I see 'tis raining. May I take thy cloak?"

"Allow me to guess," I answered with a grin. "Steel? Never have I seen such a servant."

"Aye, steel," Azurene answered. "He and the others that are located about my property are a gift. They protect and serve me. I require privacy, as you now know, and they cannot be tortured or killed like living guards."

"Pardon. I shall return anon with the towels," Humble said. He removed our wet cloaks then bowed, after which it left as ordered.

An impressive collection of maces and staffs decorated the walls in the front hallway. As a ravenknight, I was fascinated by the craftsmanship and any tale connected with the weapons. Azurene pointed out a few of her favourites, stroking one of the morning stars with her fingertips as if 'twas a delicate flower. Her nails were long and I could imagine the pain they could render depending on how she used them.

"Aye, they are all magical and I am adept at using them," the priestess said, afore I could ask. "I acquired them in my travels hither and yon; places I ventured to afore I took the position of High Priestess at the cathedral."

"Never have I seen such a collection. I best behave myself, milady," I joked in reply.

"Indeed." She grinned back at me. "Follow me and mind what you touch inside. We have just met and I wish you no harm ... for now."

It sounded as if she was jesting, but I was not taking any chances. "Of course, milady. Lead on."

Once we entered the large sitting room, I stopped to admire the paintings, tapestries and wood-carved furniture. The fireplace was lit with a crackling fire that made me wish to draw closer, but I would not leave her side. This was definitely a lady's abode, sweet smelling with feminine touches of hand-made lace and vases filled with white and purple roses.

To my surprise, Azurene bade me remove my armour. Naturally, I was quite willing to oblige her if by doing so I could stay longer than anticipated. She lit more candles around the room afore returning to stand afore me. I must have been a dreadful sight, all wet and my straight white hair hanging over my face, but I could not resist smiling. Her eyes met mine but for a moment as she smiled back, whereupon she took my helm and unhooked my gauntlets. Without a doubt, she was the loveliest squire to ever assist me in this task. Her closeness felt natural and surprisingly familiar. I found myself wanting to trust her so much I submitted myself to her care. I said naught whilst she removed my sword belt, surcoat, armour plates and boots.

Finally, when I was down to my padded doublet, leggings and stockings, Humble arrived with the towels. His silvery frame glistened in the firelight as he offered me a soft dry towel.

"My thanks, Humble," Azurene said. "You are dismissed until the morrow."

"Good den, milady... Sir Larolin." Humble bowed then returned to the kitchen.

I nodded. "Good den."

Azurene dried her long silvery tresses that fell down to her waist. She quickly took off her slippers and wet stockings without revealing too much. I could not stop from smiling whilst I noticed she was doing her best to ignore me. She was a delight to my eyes as she made herself more comfortable. When she was done, she guided me to the couch.

I admit I did wonder if she was somehow testing my resolve. Thoughts and notions filled my head when she proceeded to dry my face and hair, then she loosened my doublet's front laces. We were so close, I wanted to take her in my arms right then, but remembered what I had promised earlier.

This was the High Priestess of Espion, not some flirtatious wench at a local tavern. Nay, I had to control my hunger for her and silently recite some military regulations if I had to. I even glanced at the fire whilst I sat still, noticing how she smelt of lavender. That blessed moment 'twas not unlike being in a forest watching a lovely doe calmly feeding only a few feet away. One false move and the deer would flee from sight, or in this instance, Azurene would throw me out. And so I sat and waited until she finished and handed me the towel.

"Tea? Wine? Alas, I have no ale," she said, grinning and looking a bit embarrassed.

"I wish to talk about Brother Tomiss, priestess."

"Be at ease, Krymson. I am in sore need of hot tea. Do join me. It shan't take long."

"As you wish, milady."

I watched her walk gracefully into the next room to fill her tea kettle. When she returned, she heated the water in the fireplace and added some tea leaves. I patiently waited as she began to brush out her long damp hair by the fire. The firelight's glow framed her silhouette like an aura. I was utterly mesmerized, until I heard the water in the pot boil. The spell was broken. Once the tea was ready, she poured two cups and handed me one, then joined me on the couch.

The memory of that night still lingers in my mind with crystal clarity. The candles glowed around us, casting soft shadows. She looked so dramatic with her dark azure eyes and tempting lips, the colour of wine. I longed to touch her soft platinum tresses that shone in the firelight, adorned with golden combs. The scented oil she used made it difficult to stay focused.

"Tomiss is a druid like me, but he has a charm that will allow him to appear as a dark elf. He lived here in Espion afore humans were executed at Ludovique's command. I bid you to forgive us for not telling you of his illusion, but we could not risk being overheard either in the cathedral or in public. Tomiss chose that moment precisely to disappear safely. He knew I would explain later."

"I see. Tell me more, milady."

"Brother Tomiss helps me and others on our mission to save as many lives as we can." Azurene paused and looked down. Pounding her fist into her palm, she gritted her teeth and continued, "Each time I have to praise that ... that ... monster Ludovique, I imagine taking my staff and casting fireballs at his altar. How dare he desecrate the one we had of the Mother Goddess, but I could do naught to stop him. His powers were ... are formidable to say the least.

"And those nightmarish creatures that escort him like guards are just as powerful even though they appear to be naught more than human bats. I have seen what they can do. As High Priestess, I am endowed with special gifts few Tiaerans possess, but these daimonae make me question my chances in subduing one of them. Not that killing one would matter when our people have been led astray by Ludovique's promises and lies, but I shan't lose faith in the Mother Goddess, Astria,"

Azurene asserted. Her eyes met mine. "She created us and we all belong to her, and not this Ludovique Firebrand."

"I must agree." I nodded and looked away in shame. "I confess that as a ravenknight I have carried out orders to kill and murder in the name of the new god, but I have had enough. I can do this no longer and sorely regret all that I have done. The lives I have taken now haunt me in my dreams. As dark elves, we are above such cold-blooded killing, or at least we once were. What has become of our leaders? Do they really think this Ludovique is going to make our lives better? All I see now is fear and sorrow even as our citizens pray to him at the cathedral. And what has become of the goddess? Why does she not stop him? Could he be more powerful than she? If this is so, we must help her and her servants somehow. We should seek a way to stop him afore 'tis too late! And may Goddess Astria forgive me, milady, and give me the chance to repent."

"Azurene," she corrected me. "Here, in private, I would have you call me Azurene."

"As you will, Azurene. And I would ..."

"You hope that Astria gives you peace for thy confession?" she interrupted. "You shall know anon as to whether the goddess has forgiven you, sir. You see, I know you have orders to arrest traitors. This would mean me, for as long as I remain here as a high priestess, I shall continue to use my station to save innocents and to thwart Ludovique at every opportunity. You speak much about how you want to stop Ludovique, but only time and thy actions hereafter shall reveal if you are true and trustworthy."

"Krymson." I turned to face her again. Her words upon my ears did inflame my desire for her. "And as for my orders, I would have you safe and free, milady ... Azurene."

"Then you are with us? You would join those of us who remain faithful to the goddess, doing her will in Espion under the nose of Ludovique, even if it may mean Eternal Death?"

"Indeed, Azurene. Knowing what I know now there seems little choice in the matter. I cannot let you continue to risk thy life without my help. I could not bear something going wrong and you discovered by another who ...." I could not continue. The thought was too dreadful to express.

"Who cares not as you do?" She blushed and looked away. "I have noticed the way you look at me."

"I have known of you for quite some time, but I never dreamt you would be so fair and brave. I sorely regret the time lost over my lack of faith and willingness to attend church services. Had I known you were such a beauty, I would have become a zealous follower of the goddess much sooner, just to be in thy presence and mayhap find a way to meet with you thus ... alone."

Azurene blushed and grinned. "I highly doubt the goddess would have approved, Krymson. I should not, but I would be lying if I said I was not pleased to have met you this evening. And now that we have met, what shall I do with you?"

"Dear lady, I offer you not just my sword and magic, but my loyalty. Whilst we remain in Espion, we can help others to escape ... together, if it pleases you. Grant me the time to prove to you and thy comrades I am trustworthy and stalwart in thy quest to vanquish Ludovique and his minions."

"As you will," she answered. " 'Twould be most useful to have a ravenknight helping us. But I do wish to know more about you. I do not wish to leave my home and mayhap you can help."

I leaned closer to her and noticed she did not withdraw from me. Her lips were so close to mine. "Alas, if 'tis within my power, it shall come to pass. I shan't make false promises so hear me well, one day we may have to leave Sangrey," I said in almost a whisper.

"Nay!" Azurene answered in a stern voice. She sat up quickly. "May the Mother Goddess come and smite this evil from our realm afore I must leave." She clasped her hands together and closed her eyes for a moment. "Sangrey is our homeland. I have my family here as well. I would stay hither forevermore."

At the risk of breaking my promise and offending her, I reached over and touched her shoulder gently. " 'Tis plain to see I shall have to find a way to keep us here. In the meantime, I shall be at the cathedral and by thy side whenever possible. Ludovique shall fail one day. I do swear by my sword, it shall come to pass, Azurene."

I must have sounded like some kind of prophet and noticed she was looking at my hand on her shoulder. She did not look pleased so I removed it quickly and looked down, expecting harsh words and a well-deserved demonstration of her wrath. But my foretellings must have been most amusing.

Azurene grinned as she reached up with one hand and lifted my chin so our eyes met again. She had such a lovely smile and I could feel the heat rising from our bodies. She then surprised me with a soft kiss, our lips grazing against one another. Oh, such a blissful kiss that made my head swim when I closed my eyes. 'Twas all I could do to control my passion that threatened to overwhelm the two of us. Her lips were so soft ... so sweet.

Take heed! I chided myself inwardly. I gave my word! She might blast me out the door once again and this time I have no armour on!

Was that my conscience or the goddess watching us from above? I knew not, but I heeded the warning and gently placed my hands on her arms to slowly put some space betwixt us. Methinks she understood why I did that, and so we sat and calmly drank our tea once again, gazing on one another anew. Minutes passed in silence as we watched the fire flickering in the hearth.

"At the risk of winning and losing you in one evening," I said, my voice almost hoarse and faint, "what am I to think of such a kiss, milady? To what do I owe this honour?"

"You must think me brazen," she answered with a faint blush on her cheeks. "I know we have just met and we almost killed each other, but you see, I have longed to kiss you for some time. I have noticed you from afar and have admired thy skills at local tournaments. You are highly esteemed by many a lady and maiden. I beheld how they flocked about you after a joust, vying for thy attention with their colourful fans and ribbons. Many were from great families with fortunes and titles. Verily, I believed you would not be interested in a priestess and so I stayed away and concentrated on doing the goddess' work."

Was she being coy? Did she want me to woo her? Did I dare? 'Twould have to be done in secret, of course. Because of the way our society had become, love had been replaced by violence and fear. Everyone was being watched, and now she was under suspicion by my superior officers. Did Astria plan for me to find out what Azurene was doing? Was this her way of bringing us together, not just to help others, but to also find love in each other?

I must have imagined Goddess Astria smiling down at us and reaching into my mind. Aye, you fool! You two were meant to be together! Kiss her and stop wasting time! Was that truly the goddess? I shall never know for certain. But whatever 'twas, I am well pleased to this day that particular evening took place the way it did.

"Should I take thy silence as a sign of thy displeasure over my boldness, sir?" She did not seem to hear aught as she sipped her tea and looked hurt.

"Nay, milady. I would have you be so bold any time you wish. Now that I know such divine pleasure, to deprive me of it would be most cruel of you." In a bold move of my own, that could have ruined everything, I put down my tea and hers afore taking her into my arms. Afore she could do or say ought to stop me, I kissed her again, passionately this time, enjoying her lovely scent and caressing her long hair. I wanted her to feel how much she aroused me.

'Twas then I noticed she did not pull away and her slender fingers caressed my face as we continued to kiss. My lips slipped down her neck and I heard her softly gasp my name. I was losing myself to her charms, needing to meet every desire she had. When she finally looked up at me, her eyes seemed to pierce my heart in such a way I had never felt afore with any other lady. I froze in awe. The sensation was so new to me, so powerful and undeniable. I wanted her badly; all of her then and there, but ... it could not happen. 'Twas too soon.

My behaviour was unbecoming a ravenknight and a gentleman. Dark elves are known for their passions and lustful appetites, not romantic gestures. And I was no exception. But the Code of Chivalry demands I respect the honour of all females. I gave my word to Azurene and keeping that promise mattered more so than ever afore. She was special somehow. This all felt different. It was the hardest thing I had ever done for a lady:

deny my pleasure. Aye, jousting would have been easier to do. I was trained for that! But I suppose I was also trained to be patient, disciplined and astute. And such skills mattered there and then if I wanted to win her love and devotion.

I almost groaned softly as I slowly released her. "Forgive me, milady. I should leave afore I ... we... "

"Nay, leave me not. Stay, if you please. I told you I wanted to get to know more about you," she replied, handing me my tea cup once again. "And so far, I am well pleased." Her smile was genuine and she seemed well under control after what just happened. Smoothing her gown, she sat up and refilled our cups.

I resisted kissing her after that and she understood. I ached inside for want of her. After a long uneasy silence, we began to talk again. So quiet was the house, our whispers filled the room about our lives, families and dreams whilst the flames in her fireplace flickered and popped in accompaniment.

I even attempted to recite some prose to her. I did! I have no real talent as a poet, but she took great pleasure in my pathetic attempts. Her giggles were delightful. Her smile, the way she tilted her head when she nodded and the sound of her voice, all compelled me to stay late into the night.

When she fell asleep, I carefully took her into my arms. I wanted just to hold her then and listen to her sleep. It all felt so perfect and right. I kissed the top of her head and held her close to keep her warm. I leaned back on the couch pillow and closed my eyes. A feeling of utter contentment swept over me as I succumbed to sleep. I so wanted that moment to last evermore.

Chapter 6

When dawn came to our city, Azurene's door was still intact and we were still together in the comfort of her abode. The hearth continued to burn due to the diligent attention of Humble. I awoke, hearing him in the kitchen. Minutes later, he entered the room quietly.

"Good morrow, sir and milady." Humble greeted us, holding a tray of tea, cheese, bread and fruit. "I hope this is to thy liking?"

Azurene opened her eyes and beheld that we were still on the couch, holding each other. She yawned and sat up. "Good morrow, Humble. Aye, my thanks. Just put it on the table."

She smiled and looked at me. Her soft smile assured me all was well betwixt us. She yawned again and stretched her arms. "Oh, and Humble, you may be seeing more of Sir Krymson. Prithee, be very discreet. Tell no one who comes hither anything regarding Sir Krymson, for 'tis to be our secret. Heed you my words? Such knowledge could place us all in great peril. Understand?"

"Aye, mistress, not a word to anyone." The skeletal servant nodded. "If I may be so bold, you picked a fine-looking gentleman, mistress."

I was sipping my tea when I heard the comment and started choking. Azurene and Humble patted my back together. She giggled and winked at the grinning skeleton.

'Tis most curious how they found my discomfort so amusing. Alas, what have I gotten myself into? Indeed, the same thought came to me when I had to leave an hour later. I stood at the front door and looked upon Azurene afore leaving. She had a rather worried look on her face.

"Is there something amiss, milady? Do not fret so," I said, touching her cheek. I smiled to reassure her.

Her look grew very serious as she answered, "Do not make me regret last night, sir. My heart has never been broken and there is so much at stake."

"I shan't fail you, milady, in any way. I cannot wait until I see you again," I replied with a smile. Then I took her in my arms and kissed her farewell.

Fully dressed in my armour, I headed to the guild hall and spoke with my superiors, reporting that nothing was amiss the evening afore at the cathedral. They seemed pleased by my report although 'twas against my oath as a ravenknight to lie. Nonetheless, that was to be my first of many as time went by.

* * * * *

To keep my personal interest in her a secret, I often hid or was disguised as a peasant or merchant so I could be near her. We met whenever duty did not require me to elsewhere, and if I had to be away, she was always in my thoughts and dreams.

'Twas clear that my days of flirtatious merrymaking with courtesans were over. I knew this well and deep in my heart. My friends noticed the change in my habits. I no longer frequented the brothels and taverns as in the past. They even joked that I acted as if I was beguiled and often asked for my beloved's name; even trying to get me drunk one evening in the hopes of learning about the female that had won my heart. I am proud to say they failed miserably. My happiness depended on preserving the trust and love of the High Priestess of Espion, in total secrecy.

In the weeks that followed, I was there after every sacrificial ceremony, aiding every mission to free prisoners or hide refugees. We maintained a cordial demeanour at public gatherings, but at appointed times, we travelled and worked closely with our companions to thwart Ludovique's plans.

One of those companions was her own brother, Lapys V'Nae. We met one evening for supper at Azurene's abode. I was most pleased to meet him, though a bit nervous. I also desired to ask her father and mother for permission to court Azurene and discuss marriage plans.

"This is the conjurer who gifted me with the steel sentries, Krymson," said Azurene. "He is my only sibling, and he is most protective of me. I do hope you two will become friends, as well as allies."

"Well met, Lapys. I admire thy talent for these creations though the idea of fashioning a servant or sentry to look like a skeleton is a bit macabre. Is this not so?"

"Indeed ... so as to cause fear to nosey children and intruders, sir." Lapys did not look pleased to meet me, but he refrained from being rude.

I can only believe he loathed all ravenknights for their terrible deeds and now his own sister was being wooed by one.

"Brother, rest assured that Krymson is different and not all ravenknights want to follow Ludovique," Azurene said, handing him a plate of biscuits and cream.

Lapys looked at his sister and warned her. "You know how Father and Mother are going to react if they learn of this. They are doing all they can to support the new god lest they lose the family castle, nay, the whole estate for not complying. I am heir to that estate, as you well know. And now, you wish to trust this ravenknight, sister?"

"I do," Azurene answered readily, "with all my heart. He has proven himself to be loyal to the goddess."

Lapys turned to me. "I do pray she is right to care and trust you, sir. I shall say naught to our parents for now. Woe unto you should you fail her in any way. I have but to see even one fallen teardrop and you shall witness more of what I can do in my wrath. Do I make myself clear, sir?"

"I do vow on my sword, Runesaber, you shan't regret thy trust in me. Gramercy for thy help to keep Azurene and I together. Verily, we are meant to be so."

"Come now, gentlemen. Let me tell of all Krymson has done so far, Brother," Azurene interjected, trying to lighten the mood betwixt us.

As I listened to the siblings talk, it occurred to me that this could become a big problem for our future together. If we ever had to leave Sangrey, would Azurene leave her family behind? I had already been disowned by my own family when I became a ravenknight. To the house of Larolin, I was heir no more, and had no reason to challenge that at the time, but 'twas not the case for my beloved Azurene. I would do all that I could to keep us there, if not in Espion, then somewhere in Sangrey.

'Twas not long afore Lapys joined us on several missions and thus witnessed for himself how happy we were. The priestess and I also fought well together. With her fiery blasts, protective wards and healing spells and my armour, weapons and attack spells, we were capable of almost any task. We killed only if we had to and condemned those to Eternal Death that required it. Lapys' trust in me grew in the passing weeks, but he still said naught to their parents. Methinks 'twas wise under the circumstances. Our courtship, like the love we shared, had to remain a secret.

In time, I also met some of Azurene's allies, who demonstrated great skills, courage and faith. We met in a number of secret locations to plan our rescues and attacks. We used whatever we could in the way of potions, poisons, illusions, disguises and weapons in order to free the imprisoned and the condemned. We even had spies among the prison guards that were invaluable for saving a number of lives.

Most of our allies were dark elves, but a few were gnomes and humans who often acted as captives or slaves in order for us to gain access to restricted areas. The good people of Espion did whatever they could often at great risk of their own. And 'twas inspiring to witness all they did for us in the way of provisions, money and hiding places.

Alas, I must confess that things did not get better for Espion. Although the number of people we helped escape was noteworthy, we could not be everywhere we were needed.

We also heard that animals like bears and wolves were the next victims of dark magic. Farmers and merchants brought tidings of lurking creatures ten to twenty feet high, hideous to behold and ravenous with hunger. Hunting parties went out to destroy them, and many a dark elf died. I witnessed the new and powerful creatures that plagued not just our land, but the sea as well. Much sorrow filled our land every day.

Country folk raced to the city for sanctuary, abandoning their farms and villages. Fishermen refused to go out on their boats lest they met with a dreadful sea dragon. Everyone was checked for any sign of illness and healers attended the sick and injured. Through it all, Azurene continued with her duties at the cathedral as Ludovique's High Priestess.

Rumours spread and warrant parchments were nailed in public areas offering rewards for the whereabouts of the city's traitors. Anyone who was not a follower was branded a traitor or spy. Oddly enough, there were no warrants on those who were using dark magic. No evil conjurers were arrested. I could not help but feel our life in Espion was ending soon.

One day, Ludovique himself appeared at the cathedral to threaten the congregation, warning what would befall anyone who was caught offering us aid. To demonstrate his power and influence, Ludovique had public notices posted of the humans, faes, gnomes, dwarves and elves that were imprisoned or put to death, afore we could do aught to save them.

But in the midst of all the death and corruption throughout our city, there were those times I had the honour to partake in joyful encounters amongst friends after a successful mission. We celebrated each victory in private abodes, drinking and feasting, building up our spirits and giving each other the hope sorely needed to keep fighting.

Whenever possible, Azurene and I stole private evenings together. Those hours were not unlike forbidden trysts which only fanned the flames of our love. Whilst we talked, I could not resist stealing kisses. 'Twas bold of me, I know, but I so wanted the feel of her lips on mine. Her mouth was so warm and her tongue was soft as it gently swirled around mine. Her sighs filled my heart with such passion, 'twas hard to do naught more than was fit and proper whilst we courted. Every word, kiss and embrace brought us closer to the undeniable truth that we were meant for each other.

She accepted my gifts of jewellery, scented oils, fine silk and books. We both enjoyed reading and practicing magic together in the privacy of her abode. I listened to her practice her sermons, smiling at the words she used to praise Ludovique. 'Twas hard not to laugh at her mockery.

I watched her work with her quills and inks by candlelight at the cathedral's scriptorium. She painted as well as scribed many of the manuscripts she provided the church. But she refused to remove the goddess' name from any of the cathedral's tomes and scrolls, preferring to recreate new copies with Ludovique's name instead. Her faith in the silent goddess was unyielding. If we experienced good fortune, she claimed it was Astria's doing. Such devotion inspired me to learn more about it and read some of her writings.

As my lady was devoted to the goddess, she was devoted to staying and, mayhap, even *dying* in Espion. Such devotion can lead to fury and hers could be passionate and lethal. I learned this well the day I thought we needed to discuss the importance of shipping some of our belongings out of Sangrey. Azurene argued vehemently with me at first. But after a time, and after managing to avoid being hit by a flying book or two, I convinced her that 'twas but a harmless precaution should our rebellion fail. I even promised to ship everything back on my coin if we were able to defeat Ludovique.

It grieved me much to see her relent and sort out her valued possessions. She could not argue the wisdom of using the time we had then to be able to store away provisions and gold for the future. I did the same with my possessions and it all had to be done discreetly, lest we arouse suspicion.

We also had to spend time apart for the same reason. No one could see how much we loved each other; no one, except Brother Tomiss and her brother, Lapys. When I was away for days with my guild, I thought of how my desire to always be with her grew to the point 'twas almost too much to bear. I wanted to soul-bind with her, to become one in body and spirit with her forever.

"I dream about the day we can stand afore another priest, mayhap even Brother Tomiss, to recite our vows and drink from the holy chalice," I told her, one evening during supper. "Our hands shall be bound by special ceremonial ribbons and our secret love shall be known to all thenceforward."

Azurene grinned as she ate. "Methinks you are far too sure of thyself, sir. We are not even betrothed as yet."

"We can be, if you would have me, milady. You must know that I love you with every breath I take. You have but to say the word and I shall ask for thy hand in marriage."

Azurene put down her goblet and blushed. "Is this a proposal? Know you not what we face in the days to come, Krymson? And then there is the matter of speaking with my father. He would refuse you, especially if he learns we may have to leave Espion one day."

"I care nought about thy dowry and I would have you with or without thy parent's blessing. But if you wish for more time, then I shall wait." My heart sank for a moment. I frowned. "I thought, mayhap... "

Azurene leaned forward so I could better see the tenderness in her eyes. "Would that I could accept you anon for I too have dreamt of holy vows and ribbons, but nay, my love. We still have much work to do and a demon god to vanquish. I would not wish to start my new life as thy ... betrothed whilst we live thus." She paused for a moment and smiled even more. "I would have a lavish ceremony with flowers and attendants, a feast and music. Therefore, you must set aside the coin that shall be required. After all, I am a high priestess." Her tone was whimsical, but nonetheless, she made sense.

As if in making a toast, I lifted up my wine goblet and tried to smile. "Indeed, only the best shall do. We shall wait, milady, but know this well. You are mine in my heart and mind, now and forevermore."

She raised her wine goblet and nodded, still smiling at me and answered, "To forevermore."

We drank and kissed to our future together.

In the days that followed, the priestess taught me to have faith in the Mother Goddess, even when 'twas difficult. I admired her deep devotion to a deity we never beheld or heard from. Would that Ludovique were so quiet and unseen.

I could not shake the idea that mayhap he was not really the god he portrayed himself to be. If that was true, then mayhap there was a way to vanquish him. But how? He was mysterious in his appearances and in his demonstrations of power. He seemed to appear wherever he wanted to and at any time. He did his evil unhindered and I knew that one day, if someone did not stop him, he would go beyond Sangrey and take over all of Tiaera. No country, no city nor village would be safe from his menacing wrath.

And still, the goddess was ever silent.

With that in mind, I continued to send messages through the use of my crystal pendant and with refugees escaping Sangrey. I had no way of knowing for certain if Ludovique could hear me, but I had to try. So long as I was not discovered nor arrested because of these messages, I had to warn the Commonwealth about Ludovique Firebrand.

The enarch in Espion was carefully guarded and all sacks and cases were searched, so Azurene and I packed our money and belongings and had them shipped out of the country as ordinary cargo. 'Twas costly, but the priestess insisted she would take every book, vase, painting and trinket she was sentimentally attached to. And I learned how she hid gold coins and gems in such items. We sold what we could not take and made arrangements with trusted necromancers in Athrylle to take the crated skeletal servants into their care. 'Twas most fortunate that they required neither food nor drink like the living for we knew not how long they would have to be stored away.

Both Azurene and I hoped we would not have to move at all. She still refused to tell her family and worried what would happen if they found out. Until then, we lived with only a few essential items of clothing, furniture, food and coin. These plans affected the priestess far more than they did me. She loved her house which was now empty of her favourite belongings. Her purple roses still blossomed in the garden, but it wasn't the same. Methinks that females of any race are the same in this matter of leaving an abode, but that is another topic of discussion.

'Twas not long afore the evening came for me to attend the next sacrificial ceremony Azurene had to perform, I went fully armoured and armed as usual. The sanctuary was crowded with the rich and poor alike. 'Twas a long service with prayers and chants, and then Azurene took the life of a human boy as was expected. I looked around at the other ravenknights who stood at their stations and all seemed quite normal. I rested my hand on the hilt of Runesaber. A feeling that something was going to happen urged me to stay alert. My heart began to pound and my blood raced as if I was to do combat at any moment. I frowned, unable to clear my mind and ease my tension.

And then I beheld them: the daimonae.

The human bat-like creatures that were the foot soldiers of the Lord of Wrath, Ludovique, flew in from the shadowy regions high above the congregation. Despite all the candles used to light up the sanctuary, they could not breach the darkness above where the black skinned daimonae hovered with their enormous wings. Methinks they were just observing whilst instilling fear on those that spotted them.

The high priestess and the priests continued with the worship service without any disruption. After the ceremony ended and the congregation headed for the front entrance, I beheld several of Ludovique's shadow creatures follow Azurene and the acolytes down to the cathedral's sacrificial chamber where she was to dispose of the body. This was totally unexpected. Never have the daimonae accompanied the clergy afore. Why were they here this night?

I did not falter and followed very carefully to avoid being noticed. Once downstairs and after the servants laid the boy's body on the floor, everyone was dismissed; everyone but the five daimonae who remained to watch the priestess finish her task. I could almost sense her growing fear from where I stood, hidden in the darkest part of the hallway outside the chamber. I watched the servants and priests leave and go up the stairs, then I quietly stepped closer to the door.

'Twas at that moment a familiar voice behind me whispered, "Just say the word, Sir Krymson, we are ready."

Chapter 7

'Twas my friend, Brother Tomiss. Like an experienced assassin, he was at my shoulder afore I either saw or heard him. My nerves were taut and my heart was beating fast. Had I not recognized his voice, I would have turned and slashed him.

Stepping back, he grinned and pulled off his hood. He was wearing his dark elf illusion: skin of dark bluish grey, elven eyes and straight white hair and beard. I know not how he knew I needed him, but I was so glad he had come. Druids are a mysterious people with magic that confounds me. I respect their ability to heal the sick and injured, and even to resurrect the dead. I knew and still know of this power only too well as a knight. Rarely have I died, and I can count those events on one hand, the grace of the goddess and her druids be thanked.

I gestured to Tomiss to be silent. I dared not say anything lest the ears of those thither could hear us. 'Twas bad enough Tomiss whispered to me, but as no one came to the door, I concluded they had not heard him. He nodded and moved his hands and lips silently, making gestures required to cast what I could only assume were protective spells. My armour was already enchanted to take blows that would rip apart normal plate armour, but as I had never fought creatures like these daimonae, any further enchantments, however temporary, would be welcomed.

Tomiss was not so fortunate, nor was Azurene, as they were dressed in robes. Druids cannot summon the powers needed for their magic whilst wearing metal plates so they wear enchanted leather or cloth. Azurene once explained that since their power was drawn from Tiaera's natural elements and the goddess, they were limited to metal jewellery and tools, but not plate armour. For bodily protection, they relied on their powers and their aim. In battle, they need to kill afore they are killed. Such was the way they lived. I am neither mage nor scholar of the arcane arts, so I did not and still do not understand all of this. I only knew then I had to put myself betwixt the daimonae and the druids and pray I might endure the daimonic onslaught. I might die trying, but I could resurrect neither Tomiss nor Azurene, so I had to give them all the protection they needed.

As Tomiss' magic spread over my body, I took a few deep breaths, drew my sword and nodded to him that I was ready. 'Twas then I noticed someone standing behind him in the shadows, a female ravenknight named Zirann Keradur. I was surprised to see her, but was glad to have more help. She had penetrating sky-blue eyes and was tall for a dark elf. Her long white hair was braided and tied neatly around her head with silvery hair ornaments. I was disturbed that she wore no helm, but there was no time to discuss the wisdom of going into battle without one. I could only trust she knew what she was doing, having witnessed her in a melee during one of our previous missions.

Valiant as she was beautiful, Zirann's blade moved as it sang with every cut and slash. Leaning closer so I could see her better, I was relieved to see she wore the black plate armour of the ravenknights. She lifted her long sword with both hands and nodded that she was ready. I sorely wished we had had more of our allies thither, but there was no time to find them. The three of us had to do.

I turned and faced the door with Runesaber in both hands. We burst into the chamber, yelling and swearing just as Azurene was about to push the small corpse into the fiery pit. Upon entering, the surprised daimonae stepped back and hissed. Their wings flapped, lifting them a few inches off the ground to attack once we were in range. They leapt about and raised their claws as if to frighten us with their movements. The priestess pulled the boy's body away from the pit and dragged him up against the nearest wall.

I charged the closest daimon with Runesaber. 'Twas one of the finest swords known in the land and it had always served me well. Thus armed, I slashed at the creature. My blade shimmered bright with power at the black leathery wing of the daimon. Alas, I soon found out what I was up against when I saw it jump away. It dodged every cut I attempted thereafter, taunting me with its snake-like tongue and hisses. It moved with amazing speed, dancing and leaping about me. My temper flared with fury. I stepped in closer and swung my sword at another daimon nearby, but drew no blood.

My confidence waned, but my resolve did not. I had to save the priestess and the others, or die trying. As I continued to fight, my thoughts turned to prayerful pleas. Give me more strength or more power, Mother Goddess! Help us, I beseech you!

Then I heard Azurene evoking the power to resurrect the boy, so I kept swinging my sword, trying to keep the bat-creature's attention on me, watching sparks of light bounce off its flesh whenever Runesaber made contact. Alack, my efforts were only making the daimon angrier. I wanted to see how the others were faring, but dared not take my eyes off the fiend I was fighting. I could hear my friends, however, and hoped with all my being they would overcome the other daimonae somehow.

"Go!" I heard her order the lad, presumably into a portal to safety, as was her custom.

"Fie upon you! Begone!" I cried out. "Go back to the wicked abyss whence you came!"

The daimon hissed at me and spoke in a strange language, but I paid no heed and kept fighting. By some chance during the melee, I found a moment to glance around.

Zirann was swinging her long sword at one of the daimonae, missing more than cutting. I could see her frustration as she slashed repeatedly at the daimon only to watch it dodge or leap away from her blade without much effort.

Azurene and Tomiss were casting hand-sized fireballs that flashed in their palms afore they flung them at the creatures. They also cast other spells of sparks and multi-coloured lights which appeared around the chamber. One spell seemed to hinder the movements of the daimonae thus making it easier to strike them. And when the one I was fighting was thus spellbound, I acted with utmost haste, slashing its arm and upper chest.

Blood spilt at last and the daimon screeched in pain, but to my dismay, the wound readily healed itself. It twisted its body, striking me with its jagged tail. The incredible force of the blow, barely hindered by the protective aura of my armour, dented my leg plate, and I fell back with a crash against a wall. Dazed, I got to my feet as quickly as I could, just in time to see the creature coming towards me. I realized with horror that the power of the tail alone was lethal. Without thinking, I jumped back to avoid getting struck again, then I beheld Brother Tomiss sneak up behind it and cast a spell of shooting icicles into its black human-bat body. We watched it fall and once down, I quickly hacked it to pieces.

What happened next was beyond belief, nonetheless 'tis true. By my honour, I do swear it.

Afore I could kick the bloody remains of the fallen daimon into the fire pit, the dead creature simply shimmered like a ghost, re-materializing without wounds. It stood tall and sleek in the firelight with his clawed fists flexing in preparation to attack. Its reddish eyes glowed with renewed fury, hissing at us with its sharp fangs. Flapping its wings, it came towards us.

"Can they not be vanquished, Tomiss?" I gasped.

"If they can be, I know not how!" he answered afore trying to cast another spell. His magic, as powerful as 'twas for the likes of humans and elves, did little to affect these shadow creatures. Mayhap this was why Ludovique had sent them, knowing he would not be needed here. Was he still watching from whatever dark realm he dwelled in? Was he laughing at us at that very moment?

My arms and shoulders ached. I was getting tired and discouraged, but I knew I had to keep fighting. I felt sick over the thought that our deaths would be in vain and the priestess, a vital member of the rebellion, would perish with us. My dream of joining with Azurene would never come to pass and I would die dishonoured. If our goddess did not intervene and if our bodies were found down here, we could all end up in the fiery pit, and thus completely destroyed. All our plans ... our dreams were gone!

"By the power of Astria, I curse you and order you back whence you came, foul demon! Fie upon you!" Tomiss yelled and moved his hands to conjure up another fireball.

I stepped back, and raised Runesaber once more. The angry daimon attacked, swiftly seizing us with its long, lanky arms afore we could do it any further injury. It grabbed Tomiss and me by our throats and lifted us off the ground as if we were naught but a pair of large fish. It tightened its grip around my neck, choking me. Still holding my sword, I tried to raise it, but the daimon squeezed my throat so tightly, I lost my grip on it. I began to see black clouds and in desperation, I grabbed my dagger and tried to cut at the clawed hand afore 'twas too late.

I heard Azurene curse and beheld her attacking another daimon with her staff, shooting balls of fire at it. Her fury grew and her powers with it, but the daimon moved too quickly for her, mocking and dancing lightly with its wings flapping. When she beheld Tomiss and me, she quickly cast fireballs at the face of the daimon that held us. To my surprise, she managed to get its eyes. It screeched in agony and tried to escape with the two of us.

I jabbed at its hand, trying to get free when I heard a crackling sound. I turned and beheld a small lightning bolt pierce its back, betwixt its wings. It cried out and released its grip on us afore it fell to the ground and died. Tomiss and I fell with it and freed ourselves from its clutches.

"Azurene, waste not thy power and time trying to vanquish one of these. As you have just seen, I shall have to do it," Zirann said in a strange manner.

'Twas something about her voice that was different. We watched her step forward and sparkle all over. Then it came to me. I had heard that voice afore, like the crackling of thunder and the power of ... of .... 'Twas then that I beheld she brought forth a wondrous sword with stars that moved around the cross-guard until she pointed the blade at a second daimon that flew towards her. The small stars moved from the cross-guard along the blade towards the tip, and then lightning flashed from it. Not even a daimon could hope to avoid such a bolt. It found its mark and then pierced yet another shadow creature; both shrieked afore they died.

Tomiss and I got to our feet. He cast a healing spell that freed us of pain and minor injuries. Whilst we recovered, I noticed how different Zirann was. The biggest difference was the blade she was using. She had brought a long sword as I had, but this one was short, the length of a sceptre or mace.

Whence did she get such a marvellous weapon? Will it do better than our swords? She does our race great honour with such power.

The sound of another blast brought my attention back to Azurene who finally managed to hit a fourth daimon in the eyes, sending it crashing against the far wall, but other than being blinded for a few moments and mayhap singed, 'twas back on its feet and flying towards her. And it must have been quite focused on getting her for it failed to see Tomiss and me suddenly leap up and grapple it to the ground. The creature proceeded to claw at my magic armour as if 'twas made of leather, but I held on. I could feel my back, torso and arms being clawed and bloodied. I cried out as did Tomiss who held onto its legs, but the jagged tail still whipped his arms, back and head. I looked up just in time to see Zirann aim her sword of stars at the daimon we held. White crackling light shot forth, striking only the daimon's head, killing it instantly. Tomiss looked at me strangely and was about to speak when we heard Azurene cry out.

"Krymson!" Azurene's hands moved quickly as she conjured up another fireball. I followed her gaze and saw the last daimon alive, hovering in mid-air betwixt Azurene and Zirann. It hissed at the priestess, flapping its black wings, preparing to attack when it beheld Zirann pointing her sword at it. Strangely enough, she did not fire. With the others dead, the last daimon took Zirann's hesitation as an opportunity to flee. We all watched it spin around itself with its wings wrapped tightly over its body till it vanished from sight.

Tomiss turned to me, his eyes wide with realization. "Lo, that is not Zirann, but someone mightier."

Chapter 8

Confused and angry, I spat out blood and sat up. My blood oozed betwixt my damaged plate armour pieces. I cursed, pulled off my helm and glared at the female ravenknight. "Who are you and what has befallen Ravenknight Zirann?" I gritted my teeth, bearing the pain that engulfed me. I refused to cry out again, preferring to let the pain feed my anger instead. "And why did you let it get away? You had the power to vanquish it!"

"Open thy eyes, Sir Krymson, and hold thy tongue!" Tomiss hissed. His voice was low with a tinge of fear as he spoke. I looked over at him in surprise. Coughing and moaning from his own injuries, I watched him look up in complete awe over this being of such extraordinary power. "I do believe we are in her presence."

"Who's? What say you, Tomiss?" I asked, angry and confused, until her name filled my head. And that name was *Goddess Astria*. My anger suddenly melted into fear and wonder. I slowly turned my gaze back to the being that had saved us all.

Looking clean and radiant in her shining armour, the lady ravenknight lowered her sword, which was still glistening with sparkling light. She looked down at me, "Aye, Krymson. 'Tis I and naught has befallen Zirann." She turned to Azurene and said, "Tend to them, priestess, whilst I clear the chamber and hall of *my* cathedral."

"Aye, my lady," answered Azurene as she lowered her head.

She left us all and was gone for several minutes.

"Oh my! I believe she has gone upstairs to the sanctuary. The altar up there ... Ludovique's statue." Tomiss winced. We all wondered at that moment about what the goddess was going to do about the sanctuary now that she was physically there.

"Brother, if she is truly the Mother Goddess," Azurene replied with a smile, "she already knows what is thither. She knows all."

"Mayhap not all, sister, or Ludovique would no longer reign here in Espion," Tomiss replied.

"To know and to act are not the same, Brother Tomiss. Now she acts on what she knows," Azurene answered.

"Indeed, that is true," I added. "I wonder what she shall do about his statue and ...."

We suddenly heard some noise from upstairs and beheld each other once more. It sounded like rumbling stone. We dared not venture upstairs without being summoned. Moments later, I barely remembered to close my mouth in dismay as Tomiss and I watched the goddess-possessed Zirann gracefully return and walk around the chamber to kick the remains of the daimonae into the fiery pit. All thought of bleeding and torn muscle escaped Tomiss and me just by watching her move about with grace and authority. I still could not believe my own eyes, but who else could wield so much power with so little effort? Dared I ask about the noise?

"In the name of our merciful Mother, be healed and made whole!" Azurene raised her hands towards us and cast her healing spell. Rays of faint blue light emitted from her fingertips and alighted upon us. The spell was powerful and I felt soothing mystical waves of love cover my wounds. The love felt so pure, so strong as it did its work. Of course, naught could be done about my armour until I could get it in the hands of a blacksmith, but the holy magic that Azurene wielded stopped the bleeding and closed my cuts. Tomiss moaned softly with relief as his injuries slowly disappeared also. We rested for several minutes, weakened from the loss of blood. The fight was over and we lived. Once we were able, Tomiss, Azurene and I all got to our knees and faced the goddess with our heads bowed.

"Gramercy, Mother Goddess, for coming to save our pitiful ars ... lives," Tomiss said, wincing and turning red over what he almost said.

"Zirann" tried not to smile, but 'twas clear she was amused by his blunder.

I shot a look at him then remembered that I did far worse by speaking harshly to the goddess but a few minutes ago. Forgive me, Mother Goddess, I spoke in anger. I sorely regret speaking so.

"Thy cathedral had to undergo some changes on the orders of Ludovique. Prithee, grant me thy forgiveness for the defilement. 'Twas my responsibility as High Priestess," Azurene lowered herself to a prostrate position at the feet of the goddess.

"Arise, my daughter. I am well pleased with how you used thy position to thwart Ludovique. I knew what was in thy heart and you did what was needed to help my children as High Priestess. For thy courage and devotion, I grant you mercy. Indeed, I am proud of you all. I have restored my cathedral and shall deal with that pretender who thinks he can rule in my stead as guardian of all Tiaera," answered the goddess. Her eyes seemed to glow slightly, but it may have been a trick of the firelight. My memory fails me thus.

"We are honoured, Mother Goddess," Tomiss replied whilst I nodded in agreement.

"My thanks, dear Mother Goddess," Azurene spoke prayerfully. She slowly stood and lifted up her eyes to gaze once again at the goddess.

As if to answer an unspoken question or thought from the priestess, "Zirann" smiled and said "I look as I choose to look befitting the situation, High Priestess. Be sure you make it known to all who would listen that you beheld me thus. Tell them I was in pale grey-blue skin just like you. I came in this guise because I was concerned you would not be able to destroy these creatures and I ... have need of you elsewhere. As experienced and empowered as you all are, this was one fight you would not have won. Pray you never have to fight the daimonae again. I shall have to warn my guardians and prepare them. And now that Ludovique knows what happened hither, you must go anon."

"I mean no disrespect, but is that why you let that daimon escape, Mother Goddess?" I asked, averting my eyes to show humility.

"Aye. I hope it brings the pretender out so I can vanquish him for good. Ludovique is a coward at heart. Therefore, you three must go afore he arrives. Gramercy for thy service and forget not I am always with you in any shape or form I choose." She smiled and stepped closer to us.

"But we would do more to serve you, my lady," I implored.

"Nay, you have already done what you could and thy destiny is no longer hither, my son. Question me not and go anon. You do me great honour and shall serve me well thither in Athrylle."

"The honour is ours, Mother Goddess," Brother Tomiss uttered with deep respect as he stepped a few feet away to conjure a portal. We watched the mystical portal appear, twinkling with sparks of light. After bowing to the goddess one last time, he passed through it, disappearing from the chamber.

A sense of melancholy overcame me. Verily, I was changed forevermore. I actually spoke with the Mother Goddess and in doing so, my faith was not only restored, but strengthened. She was real to me at last. I wanted to stay and help her somehow, but my armour was now useless and I was still recovering from my injuries. I paused for a moment and turned to face the goddess once more.

Azurene came and stood by me, gently taking my hand. "We shan't ever forget this, Mother Goddess," she said. "We all pray you succeed."

"Aye, 'tis an honour to serve you always. My sincere thanks, milady." We both bowed slowly then turned to enter the portal.

"Farewell ... for now." She sighed. I looked back and beheld her lovely figure shimmer brightly as she awaited the arrival of the greatest threat to her world and her children thus far.

Never has any shadow beast or supernatural being tried to do what Ludovique has done to Espion, I mused. Verily, she must vanquish him afore he conquers more of Tiaera.

Once through the portal, our eyes beheld the torch lights and the city walls of Moonlyte City. The night was calm and I could smell the sea. Fishing boats creaked gently with the waves close by. I knew the port well for I have travelled here on occasion. Tomiss was awaiting us on the pier.

He smiled brightly and said, "Behold! We are not three, but still four!"

We all turned and found that Zirann had come with us through the portal. I noticed she no longer held the powerful star sword, but her long sword.

"Have you decided to follow us hither, Mother Goddess?" I asked, needing to know for certain, should I be remiss once again.

"Mother Goddess? Nay, brother. 'Tis I, Zirann Keradur. The goddess wanted me to come with you." 'Twas then I noticed Zirann now wore the customary plate helm with her visor up instead of hair ornaments. She bowed and stepped forward.

"I am well and honoured to serve the goddess with my blade, my mind and even my body."

"Well done then, Zirann. You ... she ... well, you both were amazing. Do you remember what happened back in Espion?" I asked.

"Indeed! I witnessed it all. The goddess was truly amazing. I felt no fear nor worry, but confidence and power. And now I find myself afield, hither with you. Blessed be, Astria. By my blade, she shall smite that baleful demon god and he shall sorely regret ever coming to Tiaera. Alas, however, I come with only my armour and weapons. I did not even have an opportunity to bid farewell to my family." Zirann's smile dimmed.

"Come then," said Tomiss. He lifted up his talisman and ended his dark elf illusion to reveal the short, slightly bald human that he truly was. "I am certain we can help you. Have you thy crystal?"

"Aye, I do."

"That shall help with any farewells to those back in Espion," answered Azurene. "And as for clothing and money, we shall help with that, dark sister."

"Indeed, we shall see to thy lodging this night and until you no longer have need, sister ravenknight," I assured her.

"Gramercy, my good friends." Zirann smiled and bowed.

We all smiled, or at least tried to. I know not how the others felt, but sorrow still filled my heart. We had escaped with our lives after doing battle with Ludovique's daimonae, thanks to the intervention of the goddess. And we had saved more than 700 prisoners and refugees from Espion. Yet my heart was heavy over those we left behind in the hands of the malefactor, Ludovique Firebrand. I turned to see Azurene weeping silently, deep in her thoughts.

The four of us stepped to the edge of the pier and looked across the sea in the direction of Sangrey, our country no more.

"All things have their time, my friends," said Brother Tomiss. "Ponder this! We are some of the few souls on Tiaera that have actually seen and fought beside the Mother Goddess and lived to tell about it. She herself saved our sorry hides from those shadow creatures."

"At the risk of her blasting me with one of her lightning bolts, I must ask you both. Why did you make a portal? Why did she not just send us hither herself? Can she not do that, being a goddess? No disrespect, my lady." I quickly looked up at the night sky and winced.

Tomiss chuckled softly. "I have learned that she never does for us whatever we can do for ourselves. I believe 'tis to keep us from becoming lazy or too dependent on her." His words made sense, and I realized I still had much to learn about our goddess.

The druid suddenly frowned, "Oh! Afore we head go to the city, we shall have to do something about thine armour. Take off thy gauntlets and helmets; I have a sack here somewhere." Tomiss patted himself until he drew forth a folded woollen sack. Zirann and I placed those armour pieces therein. The druids then gave us their cloaks to cover the rest of our armour.

"My thanks, Brother Tomiss," I said, slinging the sack over my shoulder and pulling my cloak closed. " 'Tis likely we ravenknights are not much welcome hither."

"Indeed. Come now! I know a good place where we can rest for the night. The Emerald Mine Inn is yonder, not afar." He smiled and beckoned for us to follow. Zirann hastened to him as he led the way towards the city gates.

I turned and realized Azurene was not following, but stood facing the sea. I walked to her and set down the sack. Gently, I placed my hands on my beloved's shoulders and laid my head next to hers as we both continued to look out across the ocean towards Sangrey.

She was weeping and I knew not what to do, so I tried to comfort her. "Milady, shed no more tears. Our life thither may be over, but at least we are now free, and still together."

"Aye, 'tis so. Forgive me," she said, nodding as she dried her eyes. "I should rejoice and be grateful, but my family still remains in Espion. Oh Krymson, I shall miss them sorely. I shall write Lapys to explain what has come to pass. Now is the time for them to know everything. No more secrets. May they realize that land and castles are not worth having if it means they must abide under Ludovique's tyranny."

"Indeed, my love. I shall do whatever I can to bring them hither. You know full well they have but to ask, and we shall find a way."

"Aye, I know. I have faith we shall figure out a way. For now, my place is here with you, my beloved. Henceforth, we shall live our new life together in Athrylle."

"Agreed." I was stunned. She had never called me that afore. I took her in my arms and nodded. I tried to think of something clever or romantic in response, but naught came to mind. So I simply turned her lovely face to me and kissed her. 'Twas our first kiss as free dark elves, no longer under the command of the Ravenknights of Espion, the city council and above all, Ludovique Firebrand.

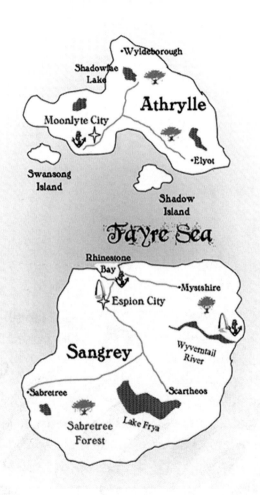

Chapter 9

Moonlyte City and its port were much like what Rhinestone Bay once was: populated with humans, gnomes, dwarves and elves in the port area. Though 'twas evening, I could still see some of them finishing up their work for the day. Ships from all over the world docked at the massive piers bringing sailors home to awaiting loved ones. Travellers of all races walked or road on horseback towards the city. Others travelled by carts or wagons, pulled by horses, dogs or oxen. Many looked tired and hungry, eager to get within the city walls as were we.

The dirt road to Moonlyte was wide, sloping up the hill and lined on both sides by trees and lamp posts. There were a few children, presumably orphans, who still begged for coins as they walked amongst us. Once through the main city gate, the city lamplighters lit up the main streets, and youths carrying torches offered to escort people through the unlit streets for a small fee.

We readily recognized a number of refugees closing up their shops. Some of them bowed humbly to us when our paths met. Many that had escaped the tyranny of Ludovique had started new lives, practicing their trades and working in the service of others to provide for their families.

Brother Tomiss introduced us to some of the city guards to gain entrance into the inner realms of the market district where he led us to an inn called *The Emerald Mine Inn*. 'Twas large and rather noisy. Patrons talked, sang and drank merrily. Some just sat quietly eating, watching the fire roaring in the large stone hearth. All the tables were occupied so the four of us strode to the bar. The smell of roasting pig reminded me I had not eaten in a while. The innkeeper therein was a wood elf named Liam Teves. His barmaid turned out to be the young wood elf Azurene had rescued that fateful night we met in the chamber beneath the cathedral. She was quite delighted to see us and came running into Azurene's arms in welcome. The two chatted for a few minutes while Tomiss found us an empty table to occupy.

"We have a room for the night. They are preparing it for us anon," said Azurene. She took her seat and smiled.

I saw the wood elf run upstairs with towels and linen in her arms. No doubt, it was her way of showing my lady her appreciation for her escape from Sangrey and Ludovique. The barkeep refused to take any money from us also.

"Thy coin is no good hither, milord," he said as he placed down a platter of roasted pork smothered in spices and potatoes. "Sondra is like my own daughter and she told me everything about what milady did to rescue her. We here at my humble establishment are indebted to you. I shall return with the drinks anon."

Azurene blushed. " 'Twas my honour indeed. I wish I could have saved more."

"We shan't stop helping others, beloved." I said, reaching out to take her hand.

"Aye, we shall just do it from hither or wherever the goddess sends us next," added Tomiss.

"Aye! We shall eat and drink to the goddess!" said Zirann.

We all agreed wholeheartedly. The mood lightened when the drinks came. The food was good, hot and plentiful. After dining, we went upstairs. We had to share one room that had only two beds which was fortunate for us. I know in most places, inn guests were often forced to share a room with total strangers and usually found themselves sleeping on the floor if the beds were already taken. Azurene and Zirann shared one bed whilst Tomiss and I, the other.

The next day, Brother Tomiss made his way back to his order, and the ladies and I went to the marketplace for supplies and new clothes. The three of us abided at the inn for a few days in relative safety and comfort.

* * * * *

As we expected, once word of our arrival reached the city's ruler, High Lord Josef Wylder, we were summoned to his palace. Dressed in our finest garments, the three of us were presented at court not only to the High Lord of Moonlyte, but other rulers of the Commonwealth.

The meeting involved mostly the customary questioning of what was taking place in Espion City. Azurene and I warned that Ludovique Firebrand was not one to settle for a single country as his domain. We spoke about his daimonae and the incredible power they wielded that only the goddess could vanquish.

Zirann spoke of the abnormal creatures and undead as a blight in the countryside outside the city. "We have been able to vanquish many of these malicious beasts with our magic weapons. But alas, more show up in other animals like a plague. No one seems to be immune to the effects of this evil magic. It could be Ludovique's doing or some of his followers who are alchemists or conjurers."

"We know of these unnatural beasts you speak of, Dame Keradur," the high lord answered. "I have ordered all ships to be carefully checked upon docking at any of our ports. Sir Larolin's messages reached us and we are taking precautions."

"Indeed," added Chieftain Aldwolf of Arcwynd. "We also agreed to check all who travel by the two enarchs in Kyngeston and Arcwynd. Anything suspicious in the way of dark magic is immediately confiscated and the individual is held for questioning."

We cautioned the Commonwealth rulers to prepare, for Athrylle may be next. They listened and assured us that their military guilds and armies were working to improve their weapons and magic should he attempt any hostile action.

"It shan't be enough, High Lord," I said.

"Then we shall have to keep trying, not just as a country, but as a Commonwealth. Sir Larolin and Dame Keradur, whilst you are with us, you can assist with training to do battle against these daimonae. Priestess V'Nae, I would have you help our sages and priests to improve our magic. You are our closest link to the guardians of this world and the goddess herself. Whatever we have is thine for the defence of our people. Fie me! As long as I draw breath, Athrylle shan't fall to this ... this Disciple of Wrath. Those of us who worship the Mother Goddess shall remain steadfast and strong now and forevermore." High Lord Wylder gestured to his commanding officers and mages close by.

The other rulers present nodded and raised their voices, "Here, here!"

"The goddess shall send her guardians to protect us as she has in the past, but there is much we can still do for ourselves. Count on Lythopia and Vawdrey to do their part to help," Queen Viola

Celeste said. "We can provide fighters and archers, healers, wizards and tinkers."

"Arcwynd shall help! We can provide ores, minerals and crystals, not to mention fighters," interjected Chieftain Aldwolf. The passionate dwarf stood up and raised a fist.

"Indeed, all of the country of Naelos shall join in this cause. Velanth's faes and elves shall help as scouts, fighters, archers, magicians and builders," added King Willon. The elven ruler nodded, barely showing any emotion. "We shall seek out the forest and air nymphs for their aid also."

"A brilliant idea, King Willon! We must not forget the elemental guardians that can help us if we but seek them out," High Lord Wylder said as he gestured to a scribe writing notes.

"And forget not the snow elves and the Wynterlanders," added Queen Celeste. "Their magic is unlike anything we have south of that continent of ice. 'Twould be wise to ask for their help also."

"Then 'tis settled. We shall feast this night and begin planning on the morrow," said the high lord.

"Prithee, High Lord and High Lady Wylder," Azurene spoke up and then blushed with a delicate smile. "We are honoured to help, but should we not first pledge our fealty and join a suitable guild or order? We are but foreigners in this land. I am ready to serve you as befitting a priestess of the Mother Goddess." My lady lowered her head humbly as she spoke. I was touched by her supplication as I hoped the nobles around us would be.

High Lady Dalya Wylder was flattered that she was included in the request. She touched her husband's hand and smiled her approval. "But are you not a high priestess, druidess? We shall find you a suitable place in our cathedral, I am sure. Have you found proper lodging?"

"We have, High Lady. We are abiding at *The Emerald Mine Inn*," answered Zirann with a slight bow. "We wish to settle here in Athrylle."

"How say you? Nay, I would have you stay with us until you have a place more suitable and befitting thy station," the high lady retorted, trying not to make it a command.

"Indeed," The high lord grinned and nodded. "If you are certain you wish to remain in Athrylle, come forth and kneel afore me, Sir Krymson Larolin, Priestess Azurene V'Nae and Dame Zirann Keradur."

I looked over at Azurene and Zirann afore stepping forward. Their smiles affirmed this was what they desired. The high lord stood up and held out his bejewelled hand. A steward approached and presented him an elaborately embellished sceptre of rubies, diamonds and gold.

Solemnly, and in the presence of the court's officers, guests and clergy, we stepped towards the dais and knelt together afore High Lord Wylder to pledge our fealty and service to our new sovereigns.

When High Lady Wylder learned that the priestess and I were not soul-bound, she placed us in separate quarters as was proper and fitting. Zirann and I got quarters normally assigned to knights of the realm. My room was clean and I was able to get my armour repaired. I was also allowed to wear my ravenknight armour as long it did not cause any strife with the other knights.

It took time to earn respect from the local citizens and gentry. Being a dark elf made things very difficult and I worried about how Azurene was faring. It took some time, but Zirann and I trained together until we earned the respect of the palace guards and knights, despite the colour of our skin. I suppose I could not blame them. There were moments when I thought 'twould be better for Azurene and I to move to another country. Nevertheless, deep inside I knew 'twould not change things and there were more of our race here in Athrylle than anywhere else. 'Twas best we stayed and make it work.

The priestess and I saw little of each other from then on. She kept busy at the mage's tower or in the palace's chapel. I stopped to knock at her door often only to learn she was not therein. This would not do. I missed her most dearly. We did not struggle and prepare to come all the way here just to be apart.

One evening, I sent a pageboy to deliver a note requesting to see the high priestess at a suitable time. That night as I lay in bed and looked out the window to watch the moon, I thought to take her on a picnic and propose to her.

When morning came, there was a knock at the door. I got up, put on my pantaloons, and robe. The room was chilly, so I added chopped wood to the brazier.

I opened the door and lo, there was my dark angel, Azurene, dressed in a morning gown, and carrying a tray of buttered bread, peaches and hot tea.

"Good morrow, beloved." Azurene smiled and entered the room.

I was stunned. I poked my head out the door to see if anyone was around to witness what just happened. "Milady?"

Azurene placed the tray on a small table next to my bed and began pouring hot tea in the only cup on the tray. She smiled up at me and carefully offered me the cup.

"Know you what you are doing, my love? Thy honour shall be compromised if anyone sees you here. Moreover, why do you bring but one cup? Know you what that means? Is this a hint of sorts?" I looked down at the tea then took a sip. 'Twas sweet with honey, just the way I liked it.

"Aye, it might be unless... "

" ...unless we were betrothed?"

" 'Twas not long ago we spoke of our undying love to each other. I have been missing you lately, beloved. I know there is much to do here, but I would still wish to see you whenever and ... wherever possible." Azurene blushed and looked around my room. "I know this is not my place, but I wish it to be. Do you still feel the same, Krymson?"

"I do. Verily, I would pledge my life and soul to you anon, milady. 'Tis already done in my heart. I truly love you with all my being."

Azurene smiled. She took the cup and sipped from it herself. "And I love you, milord ... Dearest. My heart is thine as well."

"My dark angel, you are ready to become one with me? I planned to take you on a picnic later this day but now that you are here ...." I knelt down on one knee afore her, and gently took her hand, removing the cup in case she should drop it.

"Krymson? Are you ... proposing marriage?"

"Well, 'twould be a soul-binding for us, my love, but aye. If you wish a non-traditional wedding, I care not what we do so long as we exchange vows and rings afore the goddess and friends. So again, I ask you, my sweet lady." I looked deeply into her dark eyes. "Would you join our souls and hearts and become my wife?"

"Aye, beloved," Azurene answered. "It shall be done. I would bind my soul with thine."

I rose to my feet and took her into my arms. We kissed a long time. Our tongues met in a dance of sensuality that marked the beginning of a lifetime of joy. When 'twas over, we touched foreheads and smiled at each other.

"When?" I softly asked.

"First, we need an abode of our own. I shan't stay here in the palace after the ceremony. Until then, there is much to do. I wish it to be a soul-binding ceremony as is our custom. I must write to my family and begin preparations. Who shall perform the ceremony? Another dark elf, experienced in binding ceremonies, no doubt. I shall seek such a priest or priestess and get permission to do the ceremony in the chapel."

"As you will, beloved." I smiled and felt my heart leap as I held her tighter.

Azurene looked so excited and happy. I could see she really wanted this at last. We sat down to eat our meal, but she just kept kissing me whilst she went on about the preparations for our wedding day.

The proposal was not how I planned, but I care not. It happened, and she wanted to be mine. 'Tis what mattered. After our breakfast, we parted to prepare for the day ahead. I left the palace that morning a happy dark elf in search of the perfect wedding ring for my bride.

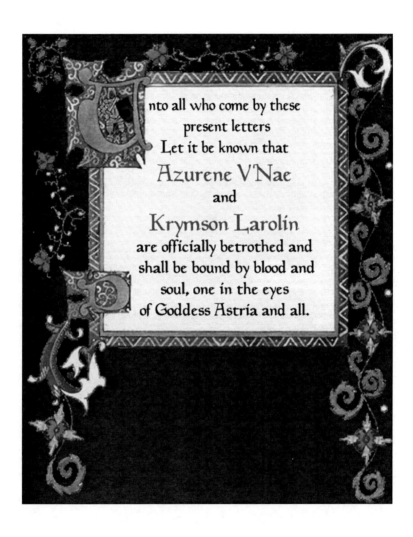

nto all who come by these
present letters
Let it be known that

Azurene V'Nae

and

Krymson Larolin

are officially betrothed and
shall be bound by blood and
soul, one in the eyes
of Goddess Astria and all.

Chapter 10

Once we were officially betrothed, and swore fealty to the rulers of Athrylle, a country of shape shifters, pirates and dark elves, I wasted no time looking for a suitable place to live whilst Azurene met with the local clergy and made wedding plans. She spoke of a grand affair that required much of her time for preparation. So I left her to her planning and ventured outside the city gates on horseback.

Naught would dim my spirit. The bans had been read and the banners posted at the local marketplace in Moonlyte City. I had joined a local military guild and became a MysticKnight. We were free and in love. Goddess Astria was blessing our lives whilst we endeavoured to serve her hither in Athrylle.

A few miles from the city walls, I came upon a manor owned by a lord who made it known to all that he wished to sell it. What ho! I could not imagine why anyone would want to disown a manor and not pass it down to an heir. Lord Dalyn Tilden was at home and we discussed what was involved regarding the land, workers and manor house.

"The price is incredibly generous, milord Tilden. Are you certain you wish to part with it? If I do take on the manor, will there be trouble with me and betrothed being... well, dark elves?" I suddenly envisioned the tenants burning down the manor house in order to be rid of us.

Lord Tilden shook his head as he handed me a glass of brandy wine. "Fret not, milord. Athrylle has come to know many dark elves who have chosen to live hither and yon. The tenants may be a little curious at first, mayhap even shocked, but if you are wise and kind, they shall learn to accept you and thy lady." The young man had dark circles under his eyes. He was pale and thin. The light in his eyes was gone. His home was shadowy inside with the drapes drawn. The wall mirrors and paintings were covered with black fabric. It was a home of mourning. Sadness prevailed to all who entered here. My heart felt it.

"My lady wife and baby both died in childbirth, sir. I have no children to inherit this estate. The house no longer matters to me. I am half-mad with grief and cannot remain hither much longer."

"I see." His tragedy moved me, but I was still a bit uncertain. "What of other family members that may wish to challenge me for the possession of this manor?"

"I assure you, sir. None wish any part of it. They shall not come hither anon or ever. I know this be true for I have offered them this place and they refused it. So, shall I take you on a tour?"

I nodded and followed him around the abode and toured the countryside by horseback. It was perfect for me and Azurene. Lord Tilden showed me the local village. The peasants I met were eager to keep up the gardens and fields.

Still unconvinced, I left him and rode off to make some inquiries in the area, riding from the house to a tavern across the manor. Whilst I stopped for ale at *The Weeping Nymph*, I spoke to the barkeep and fellow patrons about the manor without saying anything about purchasing the estate. In due time, I learned the true reason why Lord Tilden wanted to disown his family's inheritance, as well as why we had nothing to fret regarding any relatives wanting to lay claim to it.

That evening, I spoke with my betrothed. To my relief, Azurene took all the facts and background well and we agreed to purchase the manor.

A fortnight later, when the deal was done, Lord Tilden moved his belongings out and closed up the manor house. Upon receiving the keys by messenger, Azurene and I mounted our horses and rode out of the city to tour our future home. Our coffers were lighter, but our hearts were filled with anticipation over Azuremist Manor.

We noticed several curious peasants of different races peering from behind trees as we dismounted at the front entrance of the large stone manor house. It had everything we needed and wanted. There was a river nearby, windows to let the sunshine in, and a good view to the surrounding forest and fields from the top floors.

"So the house is haunted," Azurene said with an air of disbelief. "After all we have seen and been though, my love, should we fret over a ghost or two?"

"Indeed, milady. I am most fortunate to be marrying such a practical, intelligent female." I took her hand and led her up the stone steps to the large double doors, embellished with decorative carvings. 'Twas a wondrous place that needed a large family to fill its chambers and halls with love, merriment and heirs.

The inside was dusty and shadowy, but we had our crystals to light the way until we could find a torch or some candles. I was a bit disappointed that there was some damage since my last visit. Shards of wood and glass were strewn everywhere and so we were careful to step lightly. I wondered if this was the handiwork of the ghost or of thieves who knew the place was unoccupied. "Methinks we have some work to do if we are to ever have guests here."

"Aye, beloved. Now that our wedding day is but a few weeks away, there is much to do." Azurene looked up at the spiral stairway then slowly ascended them, smiling at the grandeur of the chandelier and satin wallpaper. "How many floors did they say this place had? Two?"

"Three," I answered, still standing in the entryway, "and a cellar downstairs for storing wine and beer."

"Three?" Azurene answered in a raised voice from the top of the spiral staircase. "Whatever shall we do with all these rooms?"

"Knaves, my dear." I winked at Azurene then muttered to myself so she would not hear, "Servants, and if the goddess is willing, many lovely dark elven children to delight Papa and Mama."

"What say you, Krymson?" Azurene yelled from the hall upstairs.

"Oh, umm! The wagon is coming up the road. 'Tis Master Thompson, the dwarven carpenter, with our crates and some furniture. I shall be outside, beloved." I yelled upwards to my future bride. I stepped out just as the horses and wagon pulled up in front of the manor house.

"Greetings, milord! I see you got here afore we did. I brought some pieces here and these large crates as you instructed." The dwarf hopped down from the wagon seat and straightened his jacket. We bowed to each other as was the custom.

A peasant lad tipped his hat and smiled. "Well met, milord. I shall open up the back."

"Splendid," I said.

Master Thompson glanced up at the large house then jumped suddenly. "Ugh! Oh, gracious! Did you see that?"

I turned to look up at what he was seeing. It took but a moment to see 'twas Azurene exploring the bedchambers upstairs. "Ah! That is my betrothed, Master Thompson. She is simply touring the house as we speak."

The visibly shaken dwarf pulled out his handkerchief and began to wipe his brow. "Oh, heheh ... I see. Very good. Eh ... Where do you want these boxes and crates, milord? I am so sorry. I have only Jack here, to help carry things, but we should bring everything you need today if it does not rain."

"As you can, Master Thompson," I chuckled. "No hurry."

Pulling off his overcoat and rolling up his sleeves, the dwarf climbed up into the wagon and with the help of the young man, he managed to pry open the four crates carrying eight full size skeletons. Cushioned by heaps of straw, their steel limbs protruded from within, glinting in the sunlight.

"Fie me, Master Thompson. Look!" The lad cried out as the metallic skeletons came to life and began to climb out of their crates. The dwarf gasped in horror, turned white and fainted into the young man's arms.

"The help has arrived." I smiled at the lad, who began fanning the unconscious dwarf.

"Humble, prithee fetch thy mistress. She is upstairs. Her healing touch is needed anon," I said.

"Very good, sir." The skeleton bowed and headed for the front door.

Smiling to myself, I concluded that life as the new Lord and Lady of Azuremist Manor would be interesting indeed.

To this day, Azurene and I have not met the ghost Lord Tilden spoke of. We know naught of what happened to it or where it went. Whether 'twas a desperate longing he somehow manifested in his mind and heart, or if 'twere a spirit that decided to leave the house and follow him wherever he went, we may never know. But once we were confident there truly was no ghost in residence, we decided 'twas not such a bad idea to perpetuate the rumour of our manor house being haunted in order to discourage unwanted visitors.

Azurene, being a priestess, believed the Mother Goddess was behind our finding and procuring Azuremist Manor as she is in all that takes place here in Tiaera. In any case, both of us hoped to prove worthy of such blessings henceforth for as long as we lived.

Whilst we were settling in, we kept hearing dreadful tidings from Espion. Ludovique had not been vanquished the night we escaped from Espion after all. Alas, he was still building armies and spreading his evil magic. We heard grave accounts about enormous bats with wings like flapping black banners and terrifying screeches near a cave but a few miles from our manor. Were they daimonae or just some poor bats that were cursed and malformed?

A terrible confrontation was coming. I could feel it deep inside and it filled my heart with woe. Azurene and I found a few ways to protect our manor. Animals at large, wolves and bears, were trained to help us comb our fields and forests. We knew that the sooner we found any unnatural beasts and destroyed them, the sooner we could save our animals from becoming like those creatures we beheld in Sangrey. Praise Astria, 'twas possible with the magic of our guild's conjurers and local shape-shifters.

As for the Commonwealth nations, they were working together to build up their forces both in might and magic. New weapons and better spells were developed. Countless hours were spent in research by our best mages and crafters. Such work was blessed by the goddess. With her help special amulets and crystals were enchanted with greater and more powerful magic to help save lives. We also witnessed more guardians present in various mystical forms. One only had to see and believe as I had learned to.

Because of the encounter that wondrous night, my faith was renewed in Goddess Astria. Verily, she was still very much with us and there was hope for our world. And come what may, my betrothed and I were determined to live each day with courage, faith and love.

About the Author

E.V. Medina is a medieval fantasy writer, crafter, blogger, graphic artist, painter, and Internet content writer known as Leafygreens08. Her articles, reviews, short stories and poetry are published online at Yahoo Contributor Network, Bukisa and Triond. She is a member of the Lake Havasu City Writers Group.

She served in the US Navy for twelve years where she began writing during her tours of duty. After leaving the service, she graduated from Southwestern College San Diego with an AA in Computer Graphics and Design. She lives with her husband and dog in Arizona.

Dragonling - **www.Dragonling.com**

World of Tiaera – **http://tiaera.blogspot.com**

Facebook – **http://facebook.com/Realmwalkers**

Twitter – **http://www.twitter.com/Leafygreens08**

If you enjoyed this tale, pick up the

Medieval Fantasy Novel

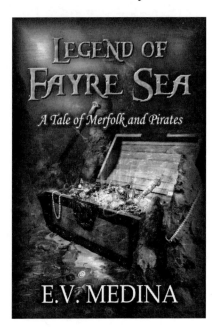

World of Tiaera
http://tiaera.blogspot.com

www.Amazon.com

www.BarnesandNoble.com

On the following pages are the first two chapters.

Legend of
Fayre Sea

A tale of Merfolk & Pirates

Written and Illustrated by E.V. Medina

Book II of the World of Tiaera Trilogy

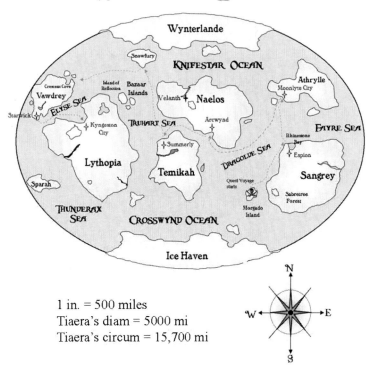

WORLD OF TIAERA

Wynterlande

Snowfury

KNIFESTAR OCEAN

Athrylle
Moonlyte City

Crescent Cove · Island of Reflection · Bazaar Islands

Vawdrey

Velanth Naelos

ELYSE SEA

Starwick

TRUHART SEA

Arcwynd

FAYRE SEA

Kyngeston City

Rhinestone Bay

Espion

Summerly

DRAGOLDE SEA

Lythopia

Temikah

Sangrey

Sparah

Quest Voyage starts

Sabretree Forest

THUNDERAX SEA

CROSSWYND OCEAN

Morgado Island

Ice Haven

1 in. = 500 miles
Tiaera's diam = 5000 mi
Tiaera's circum = 15,700 mi

N
W · E
S

Much about this world is explained in the book
but if you wish to know more about this world,
go on the Internet to: http://tiaera.blogspot.com
or http:// dragonlingtales.blogspot.com

CHAPTER I

THE WEEPING NYMPH TAVERN was the gathering place for generations of local farm folk who drank heartily amid the golden glow of the candle-lit alehouse after a long day in the fields. Sailors and fishermen often frequented there, swapping tales of the sea over pints and good food. It was also the only place in that remote area, on top of a cliff overlooking the Fayre Sea, for anyone who wanted to drink away their heartbreak and loss.

Such was the place Lord Dalyn Tilden, a young man in his mid-twenties, chose to prepare for a private journey of no return. Uncertain of his resolve to go through with this, he decided to get just drunk enough to complete his final task. He had never experienced death, but he had heard stories from those who were fortunate enough to return to life. But this was *not* to be the case.

Upon entering the smoky tavern, Dalyn chose a remote corner table and removed his cloak, revealing a long surcoat worn over a fine linen shirt and silken waistcoat. His white narrow breeches were neatly tucked into leather boots. He glanced at his clothes as he was sitting down and grinned to himself. *This attire would better serve me for a social affair, not a watery grave. Well, there is no changing it now. I am hither and shan't be delayed from what must be done.*

In the haze of the pipe smoke, he noticed the patrons cast glances at him and lowered their voices. A visiting minstrel stopped playing his lute. Avoiding any eye contact, Dalyn nervously gestured to the barkeep. The old man, known to all as Goodman Kenlyn, left his place behind the bar carrying a bottle of wine and a pewter goblet.

Stepping over to the table, Kenlyn smiled warmly. "Good eventide, milord. 'Tis a pleasure to see you again. Have you supped?"

Dalyn had known this gentle and loyal man long before he ever became the Lord of Azuremist Manor, and so it felt right and proper to see him once more. "Nay, the wine shall do for now, Goodman Kenlyn. Leave the bottle, if you please."

"As you wish, milord. Let me know if you need aught else."

No longer willing to ignore the change in the atmosphere of the tavern, Dalyn rose to address everyone. "Good people, let not my presence disrupt the eventide. Prithee, continue as you were." He then turned and paid the barkeep for the wine.

"As ye will, milord. If ye are certain?" answered Kenlyn.

"Aye, tonight I would enjoy some music with this fine bold burgundy. Play something merry, lad."

"Somethin' merry indeed, milord." The youth grinned back, revealing a few missing teeth. The poor musician had taken various pieces of wood and objects to construct the makeshift lute. He strummed the rather unusual, but effective, lute strings and sang. His ingenuity and ambition impressed the young lord and such traits, those that once served Dalyn so well, deserved support.

Kenlyn nodded and returned to his bar. Gathering around the long wooden counter, he and the other patrons talked quietly about what happened back at the manor house.

"What a pity," murmured the old barkeep. " 'Tis almost unbearable to watch what the loss of a good wife and baby can do to a man. I know not what shall become of him."

"The death of her ladyship has affected the whole village for she was greatly admired for her charity and support of the local workers, especially the women and children," whispered Kenlyn's barmaid, Lorie.

When the song ended, Dalyn flipped a silver coin high into the air towards the gleeman who deftly caught it with his hat. Thus paid, the musician started another melody. The young lord smiled, but was still uneasy. The wine was doing its part, numbing his brain slowly with every drink, making it harder for him to pay attention. Looking around, silently bidding his tenants farewell, he noticed an unfamiliar gnome and two seamen at the bar with Kenlyn and the others. They were listening and trying to discreetly glanced at him. Returning to his goblet, Dalyn decided to ignore them and focus on his plan. The tavern smells of pipe smoke_mixed with roast pig attacked his senses, helping him stay in the present.

"Are you certain I cannot get you anything to eat, milord?" Goodman Kenlyn appeared at his table without him noticing. "I have some roasted lamb Lorie prepared this evening."

"Gramercy, my good friend." Dalyn shook his head before taking another drink from his goblet. "Nay, I am in no need of food. This wine is enough. Mayhap another bottle, if you please?"

"As you will, milord." Kenlyn nodded, wiping his hands with his apron. The old barkeep never refused service to anyone for his family depended on every coin earned by his modest trade. When he returned with the second bottle, he paused and asked, "I hope all is going well with the manor. We hope to see a bountiful harvest this year, do we not?"

"If Astria wills it," replied Dalyn with a hint of sarcasm. "We all know well that naught can come to pass for man or beast without her blessing...or intervention."

The barkeep frowned over the remark, but he reminded himself this man was still grieving. "Aye, milord. I see."

"Nay, good friend. All shall be well soon." The young lord smiled faintly, staring down at his goblet once more.

The barkeep suddenly felt a sense of dread, but there was little to do about it except hope he was mistaken. He returned to his customers at the bar.

Dalyn checked his coin purse. It felt heavy now that it was full of coins and gemstones, useful for adding more weight to his body. Once he was drunk enough to do it, he would take his final walk along the cliff overlooking the Fayre Sea.

Wait till they find out I have sold the manor to a dark elven couple. The female is a druidess. This should be interesting to witness, but alas, my business leads me elsewhere.

The young lord drank until his mind was numb and his vision was blurry. He struggled to stand and had trouble putting on his cloak. Using his hands to find his way to the door, Dalyn paused to wave farewell to everyone before stepping outside.

"I shall not suffer him to leave thus." Kenlyn shook his head. The old barkeep wanted to help somehow, but he couldn't leave his tavern unattended. He turned to the druid seated at the bar. If anyone could be trusted, it was a druid, no matter what gender or size they were.

"Go to him. Mayhap you can speak to him about the goddess or something, Brother Carlyn," Kenlyn requested. "See him home safely, I beseech you. Do this and you shall owe me naught for the beers this eventide."

"I shall do whatever I can." The gnome nodded. He finished the last of his tankard and jumped down from the high stool. Taking up his staff, he waved to the barkeep politely. "Farewell and fret not."

At about that time, two unfamiliar but otherwise friendly drinkers paid for their beer and decided to leave as well. The men didn't talk much, preferring to listen and drink at the bar. Whether they were fishermen, merchant ship sailors or pirates, no one knew for certain. That never mattered as long as they had the coin to cover whatever they consumed and caused no trouble.

"Gramercy," answered the barkeep. Feeling more at ease, Kenlyn continued about his business serving drinks.

The cold sea-scented breeze was a welcoming comfort to Dalyn as he stumbled up the dirt path. The twin moons shone like beacons, guiding him to the highest point of the dark and gloomy cliff overlooking the Fayre Sea. The crashing waves called out to him from down below the precipice.

The drunken nobleman struggled in his resolve occasionally leaning on trees and rocks to keep his balance. Once in the ocean, no one could find his remains and thereby summon a druid to bring him back to this miserable life he was all too anxious to leave. *Soon we shall be together, my love. You, the baby, and I shall be together in eternity.* He sobbed as he strode towards the ledge. *I am coming, my darling. I...*

"Eh...beg pardon, yer lordship. I did nah plan ta interrupt whatever ye have in mind ta do, but we heard about what happened ta yer family back at the tavern."

Dalyn turned and saw a man dressed in the garments typical of a seafarer. He was rough and dark-skinned, and well-armed with pistols and a cutlass. Even in his drunkenness, Dalyn managed to recall seeing him and his companion back at the tavern. *Is he a pirate? Does he mean to waylay me? And at this moment, does it really matter?*

Doing his best to stand and glare, Dalyn yelled, "Go away! Begone, lest you wish to join me on my final journey!"

The seafarer's companion, also armed, stepped off to the side to flank Dalyn. Two more armed figures appeared from behind some nearby trees. Down the path, he spotted a smaller figure confronting two others. *How many are there?!* Dalyn suddenly regretted being so drunk and weaponless. *But why bring a weapon to a drowning? I was supposed to be alone! Poor sod, I cannot help him now.*

The seafarer standing in front of him raised both hands, palms out, and spoke calmly. "Be not so hasty, milord. Hear me out afore ye take another step. Me an' me mate have been pondering why ye come up here in yer current state. Methinks 'twould be a waste for ye to end it all. Come away with us to the *Bold Fury*. Thy life may be ended here, but thar be much more ta livin' fer out thar. What say ye?"

"So, you *are* pirates! Nay, I am done with living!" Dalyn yelled back and ran for the edge of the cliff when a sudden blow to his head stunned him. He teetered forward. Far below, waves crashed against the rocks. " *'Sblood!*" Dalyn blacked-out as someone grabbed his surcoat and pulled him back.

* * * * *

Dalyn rubbed his aching head, wincing. He groaned softly and tried to sit up, noticing the dark cargo hold of barrels and crates. The candlelight from a single lamp that hung from a post didn't help much. He turned his head slowly and felt the gentle swaying of the floor. Voices sounded above him and something squeaked in the distant darkness, perchance a rat. His stomach clenched with dread over the realization that not only was he still alive, but a prisoner aboard an unknown vessel. The memory of the pirates on the cliff returned. He suddenly reached for his purse. It and all his clothing, except his cotton undershirt and leggings, were missing.

"They took everything as they did me. Thank Astria you were not mortally wounded."

"Who are you?" Dalyn peered around the darkness, trying his best to see who spoke. "Where am I?"

"Aboard a pirate ship, milord. Forgive me. My poor memory is like a curse at times. My name is Carlyn Brewster, a druidic priest sent to help you after you left The Weeping Nymph, and got himself kidnapped as well."

The light of the swaying lamp fell upon a gnome wearing nothing but his underpants. He looked like a small boy, slender and fair-skinned, but with a mustache and beard. Being only three and a half feet tall, he was also commonly mistaken for a dwarf or a halfling, which often infuriated the proud gnome.

The little druid tried to smile. "Forgive my appearance. At least they left us with our...undergarments. 'Tis well I never considered seeing a conjurer about making me some magical undergarments, or I would have ended up with nary a stitch to wear." Carlyn chuckled. "Now, I can still remember some healing spells and if you wish me to do something about the wound..."

"Aye, 'twould be much appreciated. My name is..."

"Lord Tilden of Azuremist Manor," interjected the smiling druid. "I heard about you and thy family. My condolences, sir. May they be at peace in their eternal rest."

"My thanks. Call me 'Dalyn,' if you please. The less our captors know of my lineage, the better. Was that you outside The Weeping Nymph?" The young lord attempted to get closer to the druid, but discovered his leg was shackled to a bulkhead. He eyed Carlyn with contempt. After all, druids can do only so much. He should maintain his wrath on the goddess.

"As you will, milord, eh...Dalyn, but methinks that is not to be. You and I were the only ones kidnapped and pressed into service on this ship of

pirates. I would wager 'tis because of who we are."
Carlyn raised his hand and whispered some words.
Tiny, faint blue streams of smoke wafted across
the hold from his fingertips onto Dalyn's head
wound, instantly easing the pain while sealing up
the torn scalp.

Dalyn sighed with relief, but his grief lingered.

"If only I had a spell that could heal those who
mourn. I can sense thy deep sorrow even from
hither," said Carlyn. "Pray to the goddess for peace
and healing. She is the only one that can help you
with that."

"The pain of my loss is too strong as yet. My
faith in her is shattered. I have nothing now to live
for."

"Lo, you deceive thyself, Dalyn. Thy fury is but
the grief that consumes you. Give thyself the time
to overcome thy sorrow. You have lost much, but
you live and thy destiny is yet to be known.
Though we are captives, rebuild thy faith and
know that help is coming...in more ways than
one."

"How so," Dalyn asked, "eh...Brother Carlyn?"

"Just 'Carlyn' will do whilst we abide hither.
And to answer thy question, with prayer and
patience, my friend. I have lived long enough to
know that the answers we seek come if we keep

our faith strong and do our best to be patient and optimistic. I can help you for I have been training most of my life to do likewise. 'Tis why I became a druid. In the meantime, I suspect they know this, but let us not confirm anything, shall we?" Carlyn frowned. "Alas, if they do know, they may force me to assist them."

"And what would they want with me? They have my purse," Dalyn replied, "which is missing along with my own clothes and those were not magical, just costly." Dalyn slumped back against the bulkhead. He looked down at his underclothes and studied the shackles. Despite what the gnome had just told him, a terrible darkness similar to the shadowy interior of the cargo deck overcame his spirit.

"Take heart, Dalyn. No doubt, my sister and my best friend are already trying to find out what has become of me. 'Tis not like me to miss a free meal." Carlyn smiled sadly, sitting back against a bulkhead.

"Oh, now that you mention it, I am rather famished now that I have not died. Lo, but I could use a nice leg of lamb with some boiled potatoes dressed in herb butter." Dalyn looked around the deck for something he could use to free himself and the druid. A sudden noise from the upper deck and the sound of the hatchway creaking open drew his attention.

A man and woman stepped down into the cargo deck. Both were dressed in the typical attire of the Fayre Sea pirates: tight-fitting leather tunics, scarlet-striped sashes, and wide leather belts strapped on their chests and waists. Armed with pistols and cutlasses, they stood before the prisoners and smiled. The woman's eyes were slanted and her ears were pointed, indicating she was either elven or half-elven, if that was her true appearance. The man was in his mid-thirties, with long black wavy hair and sporting a neatly trimmed mustache and beard.

Both captives were well aware that magical illusions were popular amongst pirates and rogues whenever they wanted to go about unrecognized.

Carlyn frowned and sat up. He resisted the desire to unleash his anger at his captors. Now was the time for self-discipline and wisdom. If the pirates were to throw him overboard, his body may never be found. And without a body, there could be no resurrection.

"Well, I hope ye two are farin' well. I be not surprised ta see thy wound has healed rather quickly. Once we have gained yer word ta join us, we shall have Cook get ye somethin' ta eat," said the woman pirate.

"Mayhap 'twould be best to get introductions out of the way first. I be Captain Jeryn Shadur and this be Quartermaster Felucia Athlynn. Ye be aboard the *Bold Fury*. Lord Tilden, we regret ye must be down here, but once we collect the ransom in exchange for thy return, we shall get ye into a longboat and back home."

Dalyn smiled and shook his head. "Fools!"

Felucia glared at the prisoner. She stepped over beside him and gave him a good punch in the mouth. "Methinks ye be the fool. Now, explain."

Carlyn winced and Jeryn smirked.

Dalyn tasted blood. He wiped it off with the back of his hand and stood. "I have no manor. The land, the manor house, everything I once owned is no longer mine. I sold it. I sold it *all!*"

"So, that be the fortune we found on ye when ye were brought ta us?" Jeryn asked with a smirk. "Hence, we have our ransom. I daresay we be not so foolish, milord. In fact, we be most fortunate indeed. The goddess must loath ye for some reason ta allow such a calamity ta take place. Wish ye still ta do thyself in?"

Carlyn was stunned almost beyond words. "Speak not so of the goddess! Fear you not her *wrath*? You wanted to kill thyself, Dalyn? I was coming to help..."

"Silence, druid!" ordered the piratess. "Aye, 'tis why ye be hither. We need a druid for our next raid. We did read thy spell book and though we cannot make out most of what is written, we know ye be a druid, Carlyn Brewster. And thar be more ta ye, mate. I see the crest on thy cloak. I know it well. 'Tis the coat of arms of the Royal Order of Mystics. Blast! So they be havin' trouble findin' ye without yer crystal then?"

Carlyn raised his eyebrows with consternation; momentarily speechless.

"Aye, 'tis how we got yer name. Think on it and forsake yer order ta become one of us," added Felucia. " 'Twould be a pity ta pitch ye overboard where no other druid can save ye."

The gnome gulped and looked down, rubbing his chin.

Dalyn panicked and rattled his chains. He took a step forward, forgetting he was bound to the wall, and yelled, "Let him go free and take me. Druids are holy! You must know you place this ship in great peril of her wrath if any harm comes to him. Free him, lest you bring calamity upon us."

"Lily-livered land lubber." Jeryn glared and shook his head. "But did ye not wish ta do yerself in? Blast! Make up yer mind!"

"Aye, I was going to kill myself, but now that I know about Carlyn, I feel responsible for what has befallen him. He had left the tavern to help me." Dalyn closed his eyes, his voice growing weak with heartfelt regret.

"So, now ye wish ta live? Bethink you. If ye have a skill we can use, 'twill be considered." The piratess smiled, pleased with the way things were turning out. They only needed the druid, but the young human might prove useful also.

Dalyn and Carlyn shook their heads.

"Talk or go overboard!" Jeryn gritted his teeth. "Much I care what happens to ye. Lucia, let me know what they decide. I be heading back ta me quarters." The captain stormed up the stair ladder.

"Aye, Captain," answered Felucia. The female crossed her arms and studied the prisoners. "If ye join, Dalyn, ye might find ye shall like bein' a pirate. Help us in the next raid and mayhap I can convince the captain ta set the gnome free. Ye can even finish what ye started last eventide or earn a share of the booty from the raid ta do what ye will. What say ye?"

Dalyn looked over at Carlyn.

"I guess...I have no choice but to cooperate, but I refuse to become a pirate." Carlyn lowered his gaze to the shackles around his wrists and ankle. He considered using a fireball to destroy what bound him to the ship, but without his magical armor, he would incinerate his foot as well. The thought made him wince.

Felucia wasn't sure she could trust the druid to willingly betray his queen and goddess. *I shall have ta keep him well-guarded and in irons fer the time bein'.*

Dalyn thought about what to do. Before today, most of his life had been about honor, responsibility, hard work, and painful regrets as the Lord of Azuremist Manor. His happiness had been his lovely wife. Losing her and the baby plagued him with such sorrow he wanted to die. But last night's plan was a complete failure and now he lacked the will to drown himself. He couldn't imagine what a life of raiding trade and passenger ships would be like. Nonetheless, his recent past made him the perfect candidate to join the likes of those who plunder and do as they please, till the authorities catch them. *Was this thy way, Mother Goddess, of giving me a reason to live? Was it you in thy mysterious way, the one who sent the drunken pirates to disrupt my plan?*

Moreover, was the capture of Carlyn part of thy plan? You know I cannot abandon him thus! Why do you wish me to live? To what end? Oh, Astria, you are indeed ruthless and wise. So be it. Let us see where this takes me.

"I shall sign the articles," Dalyn said. "If you give me thy word you shall do all you can to give Carlyn his freedom after the raid, I shall go into account and become pirate. I am skilled in managing people, and I have some training in carpentry."

"Nay!" cried out Carlyn. He shook his head anxiously.

"Carpentry?" Felucia's eyes lit up. She ignored the gnome's response. "We be in need of a carpenter. As for managing others, that be my job as Quartermaster. I be vera happy ta see ye be willin' ta sign the articles. The sooner this be done, the sooner ye two can get some clothing and food."

Felucia strode over to Dalyn and unlocked his shackles.

Dalyn frowned and nodded at Carlyn. "What about him? Unchain him also."

"Nay, matey. He stays thus. Ye need ta prove ye can fight. Me shipmates and I shan't abide any cowards on this ship. Get ye up the ladder." The piratess stood by the stepladder and glared.

Dalyn rubbed his sore wrists and slowly climbed the ladder, shielding his eyes from the bright daylight. Stepping out on the main deck, he took a deep breath of the fresh sea air. When his eyes adjusted to the light, he saw pirates stop to stare at him. Felucia followed and cut in front of him.

"Let us make this a fair trial." She removed and handed one of her long spathas to a shipmate. "Someone give him a cutlass."

A pirate tossed Dalyn his sword. He caught and held it before him as if it were his first time. The young lord lifted the gleaming blade and waved it, testing the grip and balance.

The deck crew started placing bets and hastened to find a good place to watch the duel. Several climbed the rigging to get a good view from aloft.

Felucia brandished her sword and nodded at her opponent. "Let us see what ye can do. Ready?"

Dalyn looked around nervously, his heart beating faster, grasping the hilt. He hadn't practiced sword-fighting in ages. He was a gentleman, not a swordsman. The irony hit him that he was ready to die just the night before and now for the sake of the druid, one of Astria's chosen, he must try to stay alive to help him.

The piratess gestured with her free hand for him to come at her. "Well?"

Not for my sake, but the druid's, Dalyn reminded himself and stepped forward. His eyes focused on Felucia and her blade.

He moved slowly and waited, resisting the urge to lunge first. Fortunately, he wouldn't have to wait for long. The armed beauty gave him a wicked smile before her blade cleaved the air with a flash that indicated it was enchanted.

Dalyn swallowed hard. Alas, I am undone. Forgive me, priest.

CHAPTER 2

THE PIRATES JEERED AND CHEERED as they watched their quartermaster test the mettle of the nobleman. Dalyn dodged and swung his sword to block her attack. Giggling, she twirled and swung again. Her mockery annoyed him. He was trying to prove himself now that he had consented to become a pirate. Their swords clanked over and over as they jabbed and parried to get the advantage. The onlookers gave way to avoid being injured.

"Hah! Take that, ye landlubber!" Felucia yelled as she danced around him, baiting him to try again.

Dalyn focused on her, trying not to get flustered or distracted by the others. He took his time and waited for just the right moment to clash swords again. And when they did, he unleashed his wrath with every swing and parry in such a fashion, his instructor would have been proud of him. It was coming back, the training his father insisted he get as the heir to the manor. He watched his form and stepped back and forth over the deck while doing his best to ignore all the onlookers. His eyes stayed on Felucia's to anticipate her next parry and repost. They clashed swords over crates and around barrels, even after the captain came up from his quarters to witness the sword fight.

Then it happened at last: Felucia stopped giggling and began fighting in earnest. Dalyn continued his counter attack, and her smile faded. A narrow swish of his cutlass here and there got the smug look off her face at last. Then the piratess's onslaught forced Dalyn to step back. She lunged, climbing over crates and around the main mast without missing a step. The pirates cheered and shouted as she boldly took over control of the sword fight again, her spatha becoming a blur of movements Dalyn found hard to parry until Felucia suddenly flicked his cutlass out of his hands. The weapon flipped into the air before piercing the wooden deck.

The excited pirates hollered and the captain clapped proudly as the piratess pointed her gleaming spatha at the neck of her stunned opponent.

"I failed," Dalyn uttered, eyeing the pirate lady.

"Nay, I may just have more experience. But we shall fix that once ye be one of us. Ye have discipline, spirit, and courage. Ye did not give up, but kept fighin' till ye could no longer." Felucia lowered and sheathed her spathas then waited for the crew to calm down.

"Welcome to the *Bold Fury* and the Fayre Sea pirates. Now if ye follow me ta me quarters, we shall discuss the articles and get thy...signature." Jeryn grinned. "Well done, my lovely Lucia. 'Tis always a pleasure to watch ye wield thy swords; ye be truly a thing of beauty and likewise deadly."

"Ye flatter me, Captain." Felucia smiled coyly. She bowed, gracefully pulling off her wide-brimmed feather hat, while Jeryn led Dalyn belowdecks to the captain's quarters.

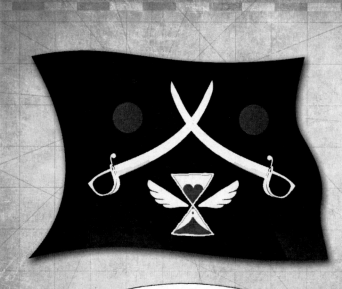

The black flag means death.

The cannon balls, and swords =
We bear arms and cannons.

Hour glass, heart, red sand and wings =
Time flies and your life is about to end.

* * * * *

It was Lecture Day at the Priory of Oracle Valley—an order of druidesses—located in the southern part of Athrylle. The region had recently received a number of druids and monks from other parts of the Commonwealth to assist with the growing threat of dangerous supernatural creatures prowling in that region.

The lecture took place in the main sanctuary of the priory and all the druidesses were required to attend. Few were excused based on their duties, but Audrey wasn't one of those. She fidgeted in her seat, using her slate board to fan herself as she tried to pay attention to her elder. She was bored and worried. The humidity inside the stone chamber where she and the other druids sat was mild, but her robe was nonetheless damp and sticky.

She didn't want to be there, but such was the cost of her coming with them to this dreary land of humans, dark elves, and shape-shifters. Now that she was a Royal Mystic, she was obliged to follow orders to go to the country of Athrylle, ruled by King and Queen Wylder, as a goodwill gesture by Queen Viola Celeste.

As a maiden, Audrey was to stay at the priory. She was one of three gnomish druidesses newly assigned there. The other sisters at the priory were mostly human or elven. Because the gnome druidesses were only about three feet tall, other sisters would forget they were adults. This infuriated the gnomettes, so they did whatever they could to behave maturely, re-arranging their hair and dress, and exercise patience with their sisters who didn't mean any disrespect. Unfortunately, they could do nothing about their high child-like voices.

Her brother, Carlyn, and Tavisan traveled to monasteries several miles away, which made visits difficult. Nonetheless, they came to visit her from time-to-time, though lately only Tavisan visited.

Audrey's mind drifted to the past when she was only a child back in their home country of Vawdrey. She reflected on how they lost their parents in a mining accident. When their aunt and uncle spoke to Carlyn about being old enough to begin work at the family mine, her brother objected. He wanted a better life, a cleaner and exciting one. Audrey wasn't about to lose contact with her brother; therefore, she packed her belongings and went with him.

"Audrey!" Priestess Dolayne barked. The tall and slender high elf rapped her pointing stick on the podium with a loud *BANG*.

"Huh? What?" Audrey jumped in her seat. Her eyes flung open as she turned her attention to the angry elder.

"Sister Audrey, where does thy mind go when it should be here learning about sprites?"

"I plead foe thy pahdon, pweestess." Audrey nodded humbly.

"Since you seem to not need any instruction about the vile and wild creatures we are covering this morrow, mayhap you can tell us what you know?" Dolayne put down her stick and sat. Her lovely sky blue eyes were almost slits as she glared at Audrey. "And stand up whilst you speak."

Audrey slowly stood. All the other druidesses watched her.

"Well? Cat got thy tongue, sister?" Dolayne asked, trying to hide a smile.

"Spwites," Audrey began with a frown as she concentrated. "Long long ago, when the Mothoe Goddess kweated ah wold, she also kweated beautiful faes. Most of the faes live in the countwee of Naelos, as you all know. The faes have a king and queen theh just like in the otheo countwees."

"We know. Get to the topic of my lecture, Audrey," interrupted the priestess. "What know you of sprites?"

"Aye, spwites. Well, those kweechoes ah naught but an abom...abomamaichuns kweeated by the dahk elves of Sangwey. 'Tis told that though dahk elves ah loved and blessed just like the west of us on Tiaewa, they gwew jealous oh envious of us. We know not the twuth. In time, as the yehs went by the wizoed and soesowuh dahk elves took faes and did magic that changed them to what we now call spwites."

The druidesses in the room winced slightly as they listened to the way Audrey spoke. They didn't want to hurt her feelings, but at times it was hard to follow. The priestess nodded, encouraging the little gnomish sister to continue.

"No one knows foe shoa why they did this tewible thing to one of the goddess's childwen, but they did not stop at faes," said Audrey. "Otheo kweecheos wuh changed also oh conjoed as if to mock what the goddess had made."

"But stay on the topic, Sister Audrey," the priestess interjected.

"Aye, spwites," Audrey continued with a timid nod. "Spwites look a lot like faes but theh haeo and wings ah diffowent colows, not pwetty or noemal. They live as outlaws in Naelos neah the capital of the faes, Velanth. They dwess like thieves and jestuhs. They smell and nebah take baths. They steal and wob twaveluhs and...and...they bwake into abodes and eat babies!"

"Audrey!"

The gnomette jumped and looked back at Dolayne, "Aye...pweestess?"

"They do not *eat* babies! They might kidnap and sell them, but to this day, no child has ever been..." Dolayne gulped at the thought, "...fed upon."

The other druidesses in the chamber broke into giggles which made Audrey blush and pout.

"Quiet, sisters. It appears our Audrey here has a vivid imagination. Let us hope that we can find good use for it afore she takes up gossiping or worse yet, storytelling. 'Tis a sin to waste one's life in such activities and it shan't be tolerated here."

Some of the student druids feigned shock while others softly giggled. Audrey's robe felt heavier as the heat of her embarrassment added to her discomfort. She wanted to run out of the chamber and hide, but that could only lead to further chastisement accompanied by a punishment like cleaning the pigpens. Sweat dripped down the side of her face as she remained motionless, retreating to her thoughts as her only means of escape at the moment.

I do so miss Carlyn and Tavisan. Where is he? Why has he not called to me with his crystal? 'Tis not like him at all. He has always been a dutiful brother, especially now that we are separated.

"Quiet now. 'Tis not kind to treat our young sister thus." Dolayne looked down at the slate board Audrey was holding and saw a chalk drawing of a pie. The priestess suddenly remembered how much Audrey liked pies, fresh baked bread, and savory meats. The answer was simple and she would put it into effect the next day.

* * * * *

"This is not cookawee! 'Tis some awful punishment and I know not what cwime I have committed," Audrey wailed as she stirred the lye water with a large wooden spoon. Her nose wrinkled over the smell of the ash drippings dissolving in the tallow water laced with olive oil. Teetering on a milking stool, the gnome did her best to stay clean, but the stench of the mixture would get all over everything close by, even her hair. This made it necessary to work outside with another kitchen worker by the name of Karyn Beeker. Like the others who lived in the convent, she was also a druid priestess who served the goddess.

"Well, did you not say you had no trainin' in cookery? 'Tis what Head Cook told me about you," answered Karyn. The young woman slowly added more wood to the cauldron's fire. Her face and arms were dirty and sweaty. She put the ax back on the rack with the other tools. Though it was customary to make the novice soapmaker chop wood, Karyn worried that Audrey wasn't going to be strong enough to do the job. Instead, she instructed her new charge over the process of making soap, a tedious, smelly but otherwise necessary task. This was hard enough for the three-foot gnome who had been sent to help her. Stretching up with one hand while rubbing the ache in her lower back, Karyn surveyed the cloudy sky. "Is the soap thickenin' up yet, Audrey? I fear the clouds are goin' to pour upon us soon."

"My poe hands ah soe and me ahms ache." Audrey stopped stirring and scrunched her nose again. She checked the thickness of the simmering mixture in the cauldron. "Methinks 'tis almost wedy."

Karyn leaned close, being careful her veil didn't get soiled, and nodded her approval. "Once this is done, we shan't need to do this again for at least a fortnight."

"Only a fotenight?!" wailed the gnomette. Her eyes grew with disbelief at the notion. She groaned and muttered to herself, angry over the way the priestess had tricked her into becoming a member of the kitchen staff. Priestess Dolayne made working in the kitchen sound easy and fun. "I am famished and tioed. Can I not just sweep the floes oh wipe down tables? Will I evah get to bake and woast anything whilst I am heo? Pwiestess Dolayne pwomised me I would *cook*!"

"*Everyone* starts here, Audrey," answered Karyn. She wiped her sweaty brow with a rag and tried to smile. "After we are done with the soapmakin', we can wash ourselves and make ready for evening prayers afore we sup with the other sisters. On the morrow, I shall then teach you how to use goat tallow for makin' candles. 'Tis not all that bad and it shall help you later on when you are ready to work in the kitchen. Mayhap you might even enjoy going to the woods with me to find herbs and other things for cookin'. I shall teach you much about how to tend the garden. You shall like that, eh, sister?"

Audrey didn't know what to think. Using both hands, she focused on pouring the ladled mixture into the metallic molds. These special molds were for making soap, never for baking. Karyn smiled at Audrey's work. Pleasing her teacher was very gratifying for the little gnomette. After filling all the molds, Audrey sat at the table with Karyn to drink some ale.

"Whence do we get this ale, Sisteh Kehwyn? Do we make this also?"

"Nay, this ale is bartered for some of our baked breads, Audrey. Our druid brethren up the coast brew it along with some of the wine we drink."

Audrey smiled, licking her rosy lips. "My bwuddoe Cahlyn is one of those dwuids. I bet he is doing that. He knows about bwewing. 'Tis why our suhname is Bwewstah."

"Bwewstah?"

"Nay! Bwu...Brrrewstah! Brrrewst...steer!"

"Brewster?"

"Aye!" Audrey sighed, frustrated over the difficulty to speak in Common at times.

Karyn nodded, glad she was able to figure out what Audrey was trying to say. "If he made this then he must be very skilled, and we are most fortunate to have him and his sister."

Audrey blushed. "Thank you, Sisteo Kehwyn. Mayhap this woak heo shall not be so bad afteo all." It was apparent to the gnomette that Karyn was going to be a good friend, and she needed such a friend now more than ever.

Once the soap had hardened, Karyn removed it from the molds and sliced it into hand-size pieces. Nothing was wasted. Scraping the cauldron carefully with the large spoon, she scooped the last of the soap into a separate wooden bowl. The young woman then took a bag of sweet smelling herbs and stirred them into the cooling soap. When some of the soap was cool enough to handle barehanded, the two soapmakers scooped small globs into their hands and formed it into shapes. Karyn made balls, stars, and seashells while Audrey made soaps shaped like discs, leaves, and a small duck.

"These fragrant soaps shall be used for face washin' and baths whilst the other pieces will be used for cleanin' dishes and clothes," said Karyn, grinning as she tried to make a bell shape.

Once finished, Audrey and Karyn carefully set out the pieces on wooden trays and brought all the trays into the kitchen where they were stored until needed. It was at that moment thunder crackled ominously as the sky darkened. The grey clouds loomed over the convent. The kitchen workers paused and a few of them stopped their preparations and headed for the door to the back garden.

"The laundry," explained Karyn. "Come, Audrey. Let us go help our sisters bring it in afore it rains."

Audrey nodded, but paused on her way out. She smelled soup and baked bread. A sister sliced cheese while another chopped turnips. Head Cook Meritha calmly walked from table to table to make sure everything was being prepared correctly. Meritha would be the next teacher after Karyn, but only if Karyn declares she is ready.

"Head Cook Audwey," the gnomette softly said to herself, her mind drifting with visions of running her own kitchen and making magically delicious gastronomic delicacies. Her imagination went wild as she imagined herself famous and summoned to serve the queen at court. She could see Queen Viola clapping in praise of her talent before the courtiers and nobles at a lavish banquet. And she, Head Chef Audrey Brewster, would have a chair that was gilded in gold and a silver crown chef's hat to wear. Audrey sighed deeply.

"Make haste, Chef Audrey! Be not lost in reverie now. We are needed and quickly, I say." Karyn teased. Then she suddenly hooked elbows with the little gnome and yanked her out the door.

I hope you enjoyed this preview of

Legend of Fayre Sea

which is also available

as an ebook at

Amazon.com

&

BarnesandNobles.com